Craig Minto was born in Sheffield in 1966. He has always loved writing and the illustrations of his stories. Writing began as an enjoyable hobby but then Craig went on to college and university where he studied Creative Writing, graduating in 2011 with a BA Degree.

I Dedicate this Novel
To Janine Helen Minto
With All My Love and Thanks.

x   x   x

Craig Minto

STEELSBRIDGE ANGELS

AUSTIN MACAULEY PUBLISHERS™

LONDON · CAMBRIDGE · NEW YORK · SHARJAH

A CIP catalogue record for this title is available from the British Library.

ISBN 9781398417335 (Paperback)
ISBN 9781398417304 (Hardback)
ISBN 9781398409989 (ePub e-book)

www.austinmacauley.com

First Published 2023
Austin Macauley Publishers Ltd®
1 Canada Square
Canary Wharf
London
E14 5AA

What it all boils down to is that you've got to do your best and hope for the same. Do what you think is right and you'll be doing like millions of poor sods all over this world are doing. And when it hits you, if it does, chance? Call it what you like. You'll wonder like all the rest of them because you've always done your best and you don't deserve a rotten deal. But that's your story! And now I'm going to do my best and see how it works out. So endeth the lesson!

An extract from the novel by Stan Barstow - *a Kind of Loving*. (By kind permission of Michael Joseph Ltd 1960).

Chapter 1

"Minton, what's bloody up with you, lad? Come on, Gaz, listen up!"

I couldn't concentrate. Jack's harsh Glaswegian accent wouldn't sink in. I'd come so far. Back from the brink of self-destruction and I was fit again! Healthy and free from the drink and drugs that were ruining me! Back from a living 18 months of hell!

"You're in, Gaz! I'm putting you at number one on the team sheet. Tomorrow's Semi Final is the 'Big Un' kid. Don't let me down!" Jack hollered at me!

The rest of the lads were great. Into the evening we played cards at the 'Brummie Palace'. Our Hotel close by the Villa Road stadium. Our game of charades was a fiasco though but we were still in high spirits come bed time. Kip came just before the midnight hour.

Charlotte phoned as I was just drifting into happy slumber.

"All's well with the baby, Gary, love," She said.

"But you know…you know…" She hesitated. Clearing her breaking voice.

"You know we will never get back together, darling! You know that, love, don't you?" She added. I placed down the receiver. This had been a bitter-sweet moment!

I'd always thought we'd have made smashing parent's for our little girl.

I had slept badly. Haunted by my past! Of those long 18 months.

The long sleepy hangover came at 8.00 a.m. Sleep had never been a friend all through my adult life. Awful nightmare's and insomnia! I'd pass the 'wee' small hours with only the TV or radio for company. Doing nothing to ease the long night's void. Vivid dream's or rather what were nightmare's just prior to the Semi Final were cinematic for me. Unnerving and seemingly real. With Charlotte's tear-stained farewell note that Christmas of 1981 recurring when I did manage any sleep. I'd been in our local. The pub we had always been to since we'd met all those many year's ago. 'The Shakespeare Tavern'. The note had simply read *x, Gary, x. It's over, darling, I'm sorry! That tender little hearted kiss within the note had become smudged with the spilt red wine she'd left. I was broken! Devastated and thought that I would never ever get back to being me!*

The other huge upset which came next flooded my restless night's kip. All the faces of all the folk I'd ever known throughout my life came along. All those local's who had thought so kindly of me. Because I'd been barred from the 'Shakey' and placed on what was known locally as 'The Pub Watch'. I was told never to darken the local 'Boozers'! threshold's again! I'd let myself down so badly! Ashamed! I thought I'd never recover folks trust ever again!

Just before waking up and going down for breakfast my sleep was broken again! I had fled in panic to London. Seeking out my old mate, Sammy. We'd been friends ever since we were 'nippers'. Always 'Larking' about! Either playing football on the street's or getting lost in the woods. Losing track of the time within our own little world's. Sam had done very well for himself. Becoming the boss of a firm in the City of London. An accountant amongst the hustle and bustle of the Docklands. He was a well-respected man down there. Always a lad to help anyone. He had been patience itself with me after Charlotte. I'd let him and his Mrs down.

Throwing kindness and help back in their face!

Once I had showered and got dressed, I walked down the Hotel staircase. My mind was still full of turmoil! I'd knackered up all I'd had with Charlotte! That note haunted me for a long, long time! Out on a limb I'd even fallen out badly with Jack! Jack Burroughs and his wife Alice had been like the parent's I was never fortunate to have known. Alice, Jack and good old Sammy. They had all been saintly with their patience of me. But they'd had enough of my creating and of my drunken, angry vitriol! The point came when I lost all sense of who I had been and who I was! God only knew who I had upset in the aftermath of Charlotte and who I hadn't!

I'd heard from Rachel Greaves one night. She was Charlotte's best friend from their school day's. She told me that Charlotte had quickly met someone else. This was the catalyst to my fleeing Steelsbridge! The emotional trigger making me head down to Lake Street in the City centre. Lake Street bus Station was where all the coaches left Sheffield. The City centre turned out to be so hectic that particular Christmas Eve.

Festive reveller's spilling out of the bars and all. That time of 1981 found me leaving home. The place I had rarely left. My safe place! Where all the love was. My job, my living, my football career!

I thought Rachel's news could well have been imagined. The Steelsbridge rumour mill was never one that I paid any heed to anyway. I yearned for the brighter lights! For a huge City where I wasn't known. Where I didn't feel suffocated by the small town insular nonsense I had put up with all my day's. I had always adored London. The excitement! The variety! All the razzle dazzle of the Capital City!

Had Charlotte really met someone else so soon? I thought as I looked out at Sheffield City centre that night from my seat on the coach out of Lake Street.

I'd always mixed well in London. All that pain of living so long in the Valley Town of Steelsbridge melting away. All my reticence and shyness leaving me! Not scared to lose all my inhibitions! To say what the hell I liked! That was the appeal of London for yours truly. Mingling amongst the rich, homeless, cosmopolitan folk of the Capital City. I could be myself there!

From Kings Cross to Chelsea and Carnaby Street I boozed away to my heart's content. Smoking away my day's with abandon to keep at bay the distressing pain's in my footballing leg's! All those harsh winters had taken their toll! Those times stood in freezing, cold goalmouth's in places like Sunderland, Crewe, Newcastle and wherever. Then I was to suffer those two awful fracture's!

Carlisle was never a ground I had any time for. On a bleak, dark and freezing cold Tuesday in December and then a fog covered home fixture against our fierce rivals Leeds Town!

"Do you know whereabout's you are Sir?" The pretty dark-haired nurse asked me. That was the last I remember of my regretful jaunt to London. I woke up. Coming to my senses I heard my name being spoken and my serious situation being discussed. A doctor who was in charge and a student nurse were deeply concerned I realised as I came to!

"No, miss, sor…sorry…sorry," I eventually managed to reply.

The dazzling white lights! The fluorescent strip lights. These were a stark and blinding wake up call!

I was told I had been found up on 'Primrose Hill'. On a damp and soiled park bench. This was overlooking the wonder of the City of London. A magnificent vista from a place which had always been a favourite of mine.

I came to remember like piecing together a broken jigsaw puzzle. My memory came back in this way. I slowly pieced together the past 48 hours of my shattered life. Before finally ending up on the banks of the River Thames in St Thomas's Hospital!

I had walked with a lass I'd met up with near Camden Lock. Spending these couple of day's with her. Drinking heavily together. Having hooked up with her in a casual manner in the Camden Inn next to the river and lock.

"Do you mind if I join you?" Amanda, the beautiful girl, with coal black hair asked. I swayed, almost toppling off an old rickety stool. A bottle of Southern Comfort whisky in hand. A glass of warm, rancid lager before me on the table. Beside a full ashtray of discarded tab ends.

We talked of our broken lives. Amanda made little sense and I must have been babbling my nonsense too. I do remember her telling me she had come down from Paisley near Glasgow when she had been 21. Having had a good job in the City of London and a stable family life. But a divorce changed all that! So now all these years on she was destitute and my company was her's. I told at length of the football, the Steelsbridge up's and down's and my World Cup adventures. Of Charlotte and the tear-stained note in the Shakespeare pub back home. But neither of our lives made any sense whatsoever!

Messy awkward world on the shagged out bench up on Primrose Hill! the following day was followed by more booze. Loads more dope and oblivion!

I woke up alone. Clutching on to a cold and broken bottle. A bottle that had been full with Southern Comfort. Amanda had flown. Covering my body tenderly with her tartan shawl.

Chapter 2

Jack's maroon jaguar had broken the M1 speed limit the next day to bring me back home to Yorkshire!

"Nee, then kid." Jack had said as he strolled nonchalant on to the St Thomas's Hospital ward.

There was a superb view which overlooked the River Thames. The Houses of Parliament and Big Ben shone out!

Shining out in all her bronze glory! The reflections of these landmarks were beautiful and serene as they calmly reflected in the Thames.

"You have hit rock bottom kid! You know that! don't you?" Jack's calming Glaswegian way had always been a great help. He had always had my best interests through his tough Scot's heart. His rapid visit soon made me realise that another stint in goal for 'Steels' was by no means an impossibility after all! Jack's face had been a mask of hard composure. But his disappointment was there never the less. Even a solitary tear began to form from the old lad. 'Bloody hell! The boss is human after all!' I was to find myself thinking with some surprise! My situation must certainly have touched the old lad's hardened heart and soul! I had never known Mr Jack Burroughs be like this. He was always so resolute and strong until that day!

Jack Burroughs had first seen me play in the local park behind our Evie's cosy council flat on the Foxley Estate.

A local farmer in Steelsbridge called Stan Francis had donated land to the football club. Stan had also kindly paid for some goalpost's, netting and erected a simple stand as well as some changing room's. Stan became a life-long supporter of the club.

One Saturday morning I just couldn't wait to go for my trial. The one which would change my young life forever! I had always been awkward with folk. Fourteen year's old and so timid and quiet. I'd heard a scout was to be there at my trial? There to choose and possibly sign four new lad's for 'Steelsbridge Town Association Football Club'.

By the 6th of August 1966 I had just celebrated my 16th birthday. I then went on to establish myself in the 'Steels' second team squad. They had certainly taken a gamble on me. A chance I was so grateful for!

I always remembered Jack Burroughs as a quiet reserved gentleman of few words. When he had asked if I'd like to sign a contract, I jumped at the chance. I was really made-up! To be an apprentice footballer with 'Steels' was all I had ever dreamt about!

"You are a 'wee' bit 'wee' for a keeper 'laddy'. But 'yee' is as brave as a lion kid. I'll be taking a gamble on you, OK?" "I remember so well," Jack saying.

Mr Burroughs certainly knew his football. That summer of 56' changed my 'shitty' life! All with the gaffers inspirational words and a swift stroke of pen on paper with my signature!

The winter of 1956 had been a harsh one! Snow, ice and blizzard's had devastated the north of England. The Valley Town of Steelsbridge was a blanket of white from the factory gate's on the main road to the surrounding hillside above.

Christmas that year had been icy, freezing cold and white over!

I had met Charlotte Manners in the Shakespeare pub. I lived with my older sister, Evie. Her two-bed flat was across the road from this pub on Lindley Crescent. The pub had always been our local. Evie had brought me up!

Christmas Eve that year of 56' had been wonderful! I'd arranged to meet Sammy and Mick in the Tap Room of the 'Steely'. This was the best of the working men's clubs in the Valley. Sammy had recently decided to fly away! taking flight off to Australia. He had secured a position with a reputable and large firm of accountants in Sydney. A whole world away from his home of Steelsbridge since 1940. In the early days of January 1957, Sam was off!

As for Michael. He had been feeling the dread of returning home every night. Those were dark day's for Mick!

Michael Joyce Jnr or always 'Mick' to us all in the Valley was so gifted. His dreams of playing for 'Town' had been his since being able to walk and talk. A fine midfield player. Football had always been Michael's saving grace. Solace from turmoil and heartache that was going on at home! His father, Michael Joyce Snr, had fell into alcoholism! His wasteful years of time spent in one prison or another was so harsh on his only son. Mick rarely stood a chance really!

On that Christmas Eve of 56' we all went to visit Mick's Dad in 'Artley' prison. I travelled with Mick and his Mum, Julie and Sammy Chivers. Through the abysmal arctic weather to the City of Leeds by coach. There was a lot of heartache that day where Mick and Julie were concerned and we were all so relieved to get back safely to Steelsbridge. Our Valley Town was such a welcome sight that night!

Once safely back home and warming our souls in the Shakespeare Tavern, we all found ourselves discussing the fate of Michael Snr! A man who had fallen far from grace! Once famed world-wide as a children's author, his star rose high! Firstly in Britain and then America! But his life began to disintegrate just as fast! His decline into the ravages of alcohol aged Mick's old man beyond repair! Then he took out his failing's on his loving family!

Julie Joyce was a lovely lady. Quiet, kind and her husband and kid's rock. A massive influence for her husband son and young daughter Aimee.

By that Christmas Eve of 1956, young Michael and two-year-old Aimee had watched Julie pack up her suitcase! She needed to find valuable space. To seek solace and head back home to the South of England. To spend Christmas and the New Year in London made perfect sense to her. Julie had always been very close to her younger sister Maureen. Her twin sister by only a few hours. Maureen was the only family she had left back in the South. Aimee didn't really understand until much later in her life. Maureen had been happily wed to Robert for many, many year's and they lived in comfort in a three-storey property near Clapham Common in South London.

Young Mick had been left enough cash, food and list of phone numbers by his mother. She need not have worried though! My best mate had always been able to hack life on his own!

Julie Anne Joyce had come to the end of her 'tether'! Needing to flee Steelsbridge. To leave behind all the hurt she had been experiencing for years. She was in need of rest bite!

Mick Joyce went in the Royal Navy. The following year in the January of 1957. Signing on for nine year's. Only returning very briefly the football season of 1969/70 to help out as player and to then coach 'Steels'. But just as with his old man, Mick succumbed to the demon drink, which left him unfulfilled as far as his footballing ambitions went! He was to play in only a handful of matches that season. Mick had his dream's dashed by a string of broken relationship's in Portsmouth and drink certainly contributed to things while serving in the Navy. His childhood hang ups had left their mark! Tainting both his Naval and footballing career! As a teenager in the Valley Mick had astonishing talent! A bright light of the Steel's midfield. Before achieving the rank as petty officer in the Royal Navy.

"Go on and bloody well ask her you 'scn', you soft sod! Sammy had suddenly said to me at the 'Shakey' bar – that Christmas of 56."

Frank Taylor, the landlord had been stood puffing and blowing out his cheeks. As I 'gorped' all 'gormless' at Charlotte Manners. While at the same time attempting to have Frank serve me.

"Come on, kid. Bars packed 'out' and I aint got time to wait while 'tha' 'gorps' at some 'lass' over 'theer'."

Frank was a true gent. Salt of the earth and popular as everyone liked him. But if the old till wasn't ringing (especially over Xmas) he could tend to get 'knarcky'!

Charlotte looked adorable that Christmas! Wearing a wine, red dress. Sparkling with little silver stars on the shoulder's and a cream shawl covering her slender frame. Her dark chocolate hair and beautiful eyes were to melt my heart!

So I was left dumb struck! Something both Sammy and Frank were quick to notice and comment upon.

"You've fancied her for ages, haven't you, Gaz?" Sammy had asked me just before Mick strode over to us both before disappearing to put a favourite song on the juke box.

By end of that night the whole pub was sick of hearing Eddie Cochrane. Stumbling around pissed, Mick collided into Frank as he was collecting glasses from the Tap Room Bar!

"Look, 'Out' you soppy young sod!" Frank said as he recovered his balance.

Frank and Mick then proceeded to have a dummy boxing bout. Like two sparring 'Valley' heavyweight's. Throwing fresh air punches over each other's broad shoulders and heads!

"Merry 'Crimbo', Mr Taylor!" Mick had cried before kissing Frank on the cheek! Mick was always great fun when he was in this kind of mood. Christmas had always been his favourite time of year.

"Yeah, 'Gaz' lad. Don't 'thee' hide that 'leight' under a bush! Or whatever saying is?" Mick said to me before bursting out laughing. He was on top form that night.

"I will bloody well ask her for 'ya' if 'tha' likes, mate!"

Mick's Cheshire cat grin lit up the old 'Shakey' Tap Room!

"'Rach' loves the bloody bones of me, lad's." Mick suddenly blurted out whilst winking at myself and Sammy. Then he dashed across the room to where the seating lined the Tap Room walls. Falling with grace. Despite his pissed-up state. Into an empty seat beside Charlotte and Rachel! We all grinned. Amazed at Mick's antics. No sooner had he sat down did Mick choose to leap to his feet again! Before dancing himself daft round and round the Christmas tree to the rock 'n' roll of his hero Eddie Cochrane blasting out from the juke box!

Mick's hair was cut and shorn to his scalp! He had been training himself for the Royal Navy. Running around the streets of the town for months, Mick had dashed around all the estates of the Valley. Getting himself fitter and healthier than he had ever been in his young life. He was desperate to have a life at sea! To escape Steelsbridge! To free himself from the punches, kick's and suffocating home life dished out by his old man! To flee all the hurt at home!

Mick was really well turned out. Immaculate! His hair cut short in a crew cut. His blaze of orange, ginger hair no longer visible because he had the most striking pale blue eyes I had ever seen! Any lass in the Valley or elsewhere he came across were smitten! He had a charming way with them. Not even having to try to attract a lass! Not just back then in 1956–57 but throughout his life.

I am not really sure what became of Michael Jnr that Christmas of 56'. I was stood at the 'Shakey' bar with Sammy as he had gone over in such a hurry to be with the girl's. With Rachel and Charlotte. Those three had always been the best of friend's. Despite all Mick's bravado he was as insecure as anyone I'd ever known!

"He never shagged Rachel, you know?" Sammy said as we propped up the corner of Frank Taylor's bar.

"He's so full of shit!"

"I know, Sam," I replied.

When Sammy Chivers swore, a chill would often cut through me! Placid quiet and so laid back as he was, where the booze was involved though. Sammy's demons could often surface! He rarely drank! Maybe that was why It wasn't just his language. But the previous Easter he had. almost ended up getting locked up! So he had tried to keep a lid on things ever since then!

"I know Sam, lad," I had said. Trying to keep him calm. Keeping my eye on his body language, Sam was as thin as a stick of Skegness rock! Always smart though. Immaculate! With neat blonde hair, closely cut. Plain feature's. No real character as far as his appearance went. But always pasty, pale, almost ghostly and gaunt! His greeny, brown eyes mixed with sadness and hurt for some reason, to me. He never seemed that happy, Sam. A mystery really! Sammy had been brought up by the most loving and stable family. His father was a doctor at the local Valley surgery and his Mum was a celebrated children's author and gifted illustrator. He had a younger sister, Mandy, and they all seemed so close as far as I could see.

So, I couldn't really fathom old Sammy at times? Not when he didn't seem at all happy with his lot!

We had been stood chatting with Frank at the end of the night. The place was quieter. Both Sam and I were leaning on the bar amongst the empty pint glasses and spillage's of the night. Opening the hatch of the bar. Frank from a heavy night of business carried a tower of empty pint pots.

"Those three, Sammy," I said almost as a whisper.

"Those three. Charlotte, Rachel and Mick. Well, they are all as birds of a feather really." Sam looked preoccupied and I ended up repeating myself in a louder tone.

"What I mean is that what with Charlotte and Rachel having been brought up in the 'Rose House' and Mick's old fellar being…we…ll…you…K…know!" I manage to just about say.

Feeling uncomfortable, all of a sudden I looked over at the old 'Shakey' clock above the juke box. I didn't dislike Mick's Dad in any way. In fact I thought he had pretty much been a victim of his own success. Hanger's on and those who had taken the piss once too often once he had found fame had a lot to answer to in my eyes. But no one I knew took the least bit of pleasure in seeing Michael Snr in such a dark place in his life and so unhappy.

"Thank God for Julie, hey, lad's," Frank said calmly as he demolished a well-earnt pint of his own amber lager before drawing heavily on his cigarette and then slowly continuing around the Tap Room and the rest of his pub. Calmly reminding customer's in the Saloon bar next door to sup up before sending them on their way and safely off home. So ending another year of festive celebration's at the Shakespeare Tavern in Steelsbridge.

"Yeah, Frank's right, you know, Sam."

"Yeah, I know, Gaz. She is the salt of the earth Julie. A mother to all of us here in the Valley."

Sammy's eyes suddenly misted over then, as he sauntered off to the gent's. Old Sammy could come over all maudlin at times. It was usually to do with some 'lass' or other or other friendship's. He was a sensitive kid, Sammy!

By the chimes of midnight on the 'Shakey' clock, I'd phoned Evie. I'd asked nervously if she would mind if I brought someone back to our flat?

"Yes, of course, you can, love" she'd said. All excited and intrigued.

"Sal is really excited, Gary. You know about Santa? She's crashed out on the sofa now."

"Ah, our poor love, Sally," I'd said then. "Who is this mystery person then, Mr?" Evie asked.

"Is it a lass? About time you made me an aunty and gave Sally a new cousin… Only kidding love…" Evie said with a nervous giggle.

"Don't worry, lad, I'm putting our Sally to bed now, so you can have the front room all to yourselves. Tell me all in the morning, love. Have you got your key by the way, Gary?" Evie asked overly concerned as ever.

"Yeah, Evie, don't fuss so I'll be fine. I'm coming on over now. Merry Christmas, Evie. Give Sally a special, big goodnight kiss from her big daft uncle."

"I will do, Gary, and Merry Christmas to you too, love," Evie replied.

Chapter 3

"Why not ask me before now?" Charlotte had asked as we sat in Evie's flat in the early hours of that Christmas Eve back in 1956.

I put a record on the turntable. The record player was neatly placed by the black and white television sets. Nicely arranged into the ivory corner unit of our cosy living room.

I had noticed Charlotte's eyes light up in the 'Shakey' every time a Nina Simon record came on over the juke box and when 'Ain't Got No Life' was chosen. She would be really made up! So I thought I'd take a gamble. Hoping this would break the ice between us both.

"Eh…Mmmm…Eh…mmm. I just couldn't pluck up the…cour…" Is all I could manage. In answer to Charlotte's question as my legs began to slowly weaken. I only just made the few steps from the turntable to sit back down on the sofa! My mouth began to feel numb and I fell into an awkward silence.

Nina Simon's beautiful voice filled the room. This brightness did the trick. Charlotte's face shone with love for Nina's music!

That bonfire night of 56' had been a real highlight for Charlotte. Mick had made a real fuss of her. There was firstly his huge and comical 18th birthday card. Then he made sure she need not buy a drink all the night long. 'Big Frank' and the rest of us at Charlotte's do presented her with memorable gifts including a massive box of expensive chocolate's. But the most touching moment of the night came when Mick presented the birthday girl with a lovely bunch of her favourite flowers. Hidden deep inside these lilies was a marvellous and sparkling silver crucifix in a classy claret red presentation box!

Some hours earlier as the party had just got under way, Mick had played the joker as ever. Presenting Charlotte with a scraggy old bunch of daffodil's. He'd taken a short cut through the allotment's nearby as a quick way to get to the 'Shakey' on time. He'd grabbed a fistful of the daff's. Charlotte's face was a blaze with embarrassment. But no one was in the least surprised by Mick's big-hearted yet clumsy gesture.

"Bloody hell fire, Mick." Sammy called out as he tried to spare Charlotte's blushes' as he came to her rescue!
"Get over to old 'Ma' Palmer's shop before she closes up!" Sammy added.

Mrs Flora Palmer owned the classic 'Aladdin's Cave' of a place. She could get you just about anything at any hour of the night or day! She had the amazing knack of conjuring up a gift, food or no matter what one of her many Valley customer's required. Once a florist for royalty in London, Flora as a young lady had her own palatial premise's close by the famous Buckingham Palace Road near to Victoria Station. A blooming, wonderful place! Then many year's serving in her shop of delights across from Frank's 'Shakey' was a true God send to our community!

"How old are you, Charlotte?"

"See here now, Mr Minton, Sir." Charlotte said laughing nervously. Before nudging me gently in the ribs. The tip of her red finger nail stinging a little.

"You don't ask a girl that sort of thing you know. A girl never tells." This really broke the iceberg of nerves between us. The awkward unease then melting away.

We both ended up giggling like silly kids. Which was exactly what we were back then in that winter of 1956.

Charlotte held her glass of red wine. Her hands much calmer than before. We clinked our glasses together! My wine ending up spilling all over the place! Over all the cream and crimson flowered sofa! "Evie will be having harsh words with me!" I remember thinking.

"Anyway, Mr! Weren't you at my 18th birthday do in 'The Shakey?' '…were you Gary?" Charlotte looked slightly worried as she asked me. Uncertain and concerned.

"Oh, yeah…erm. Was I, Charl…?" I tried to make this sound light-hearted. Jokey. But I was worried too! But then began to visualise that night of her do.

"Oh, yeah, of course, I was, Mrs! Did you like my card by the way?" I said eventually. As I began to feel a little more sure of myself again.

"Me, Mick and Sammy chose it, yes!" Mrs P had been very careful and a big help to us. She'd made sure the card would be one that Charlotte would appreciate.

"Did you like the card, Charlotte? Lo…lo…v…" I very nearly went and blurted out then. I had never even called our Evie or Sally love ever before!

"Charlotte, are you OK?" I quickly asked. I had never seen Charlotte Manners like this before! So lost for words!

She had always seemed confident and strong! Someone who was seldom phased by 'out' in life.

" I am love." She then said, "Her composure returning. I was so pleased. My heart began to dance! I was full of joy that she had called me love!"

"Of course I did Gary." She said once again in a relaxed and calm way.

"I was quite surprised though!"

"Oh." I replied. "Why was that then?"

"Well, I always knew Mick to be a real softy, you know! Under all the bluster and pretend macho stuff! He's as soft as 'out' – A real sweetheart, Gary, you know?"

"Yeah, I hadn't really thought that about Mick. But, yeah, you're right." I agreed.

"You have lovely handwriting, Mr." She kindly said to me then.

I looked at the mess the wine had made! The stain, seeping and spreading into Evie's expensive sofa. I didn't know where to look though! I began to feel the blood draining from my face! Then I couldn't help blushing! To almost match the claret red that now soaked our sofa.

"Yeah, your handwriting is great, Gary, if you don't mind me saying! Serious though, 'Mr'. I thought back then…well, y…you…kn…ow? You were nowhere near as daft and all that as Sammy and Mick were."

"Or pretend to be Charlotte." I said as I began to feel more at ease with her. As Charlotte made good the mess I'd made. I cleared away the glasses and then noticed something about Charlotte, I realised she was more sensitive than I'd first thought. But then we all put on a front sometimes. Or are guarded until we get to know someone better.

By 2.00 a.m. that Christmas morning, we had both become more than friends. Charlotte cuddled up to me on the sofa. Evie had been saving hard for months to pay for this. When she'd had Sally some three years before. Charlotte's body fell in with mine. My arm draping over her bare shoulders. I wiped away a trail of her black hair from her cheek. Just a whispering trail which had fallen over her eyes. We kissed and this meant we were as close then as we ever would be Looking back.

I was feeling like a King that Christmas as though I had won the World Cup with England and then danced all over the Wembley pitch!

One day, I thought. *This may happen*? As I lay my weary head down to sleep in my bedroom in the early hours of that Christmas Day, I'd been courting Charlotte for getting on for two year's. She was so happy and, of course, so was I. Content, relaxed and at ease with our world.

Mick settled into the Navy in Portsmouth and Sammy did the same in Australia. They hadn't returned to the Valley very often since that year end of 56'. Sammy had written often for the first few months as he settled down to his new life abroad. Finding himself digs near to Sydney Harbour Bridge. He had phoned Mick a couple of times in Portsmouth, telling him he would try to make the do for my 18th birthday. But I didn't expect him to and I fully understood this. He had applied for citizenship in Australia! So, of course, I was pleased for the lad. Happy that he was making a bright, exciting life for himself. I missed my old mate. But he and Mick had chosen a life away from their home town. Taking up the many opportunities lacking in Steelsbridge.

As the year's sped by Mick dated various lasses down in the South. As for Sammy. He had always been a bit of a loner and didn't really bother much with relationship's. He did, however, come to marry to my great surprise! A long time later.

The longer Sammy and Mick were away, the more the Valley came to be less of a priority for them both.

On my 18th birthday, Mick did come home. He had been to Gibraltar for 12 months on a ship. He said he had loved the place!

Mick entered the 'Shakey' as large as life! Looking fit tanned and healthy. Flush with plenty of cash that the Navy had provided in wage's. Having been away to Cyprus and the United States. He'd also made life more comfortable for his mother Julie. Sending her regular fund's to help her and his old man out in this way. Julie had been able to put a little away with a view to one day buying a new home.

My birthday bash turned out to be a normal night really. We all just ended up sitting around chatting with the regulars in the pub. Frank was kind enough to put on a buffet and told us to feel free to put records on the juke box. He was also good enough to have let us all do this for free. We enjoyed ourselves. But I reflected as last orders were called that we had all suddenly grown up and were now ready to face the adult world!

Chapter 4

In the spring of 1957, Mick left for sea once again, following a few weeks leave in the Valley. When he returned home again this was for the saddest of reason's!

Michael Joyce snr's funeral was a very strange experience for us all in Steelsbridge. An extremely gifted artist he had left school in the summer of 1937. His creative ambitions led to studies at the Sheffield Art College. From there, he went on to be an accomplished author and illustrator of his novel's. His real passion came through with the brilliant children's books he produced.

Michael Snr and his wife Julie had travelled with young Mick around the world. Success came in America and in particular New York. A place where the author was adored by the public. Especially children. Mick's Dad found people to be an eye opener! Manipulative and vindictive in some cases. As the business side of publishing in the States proved to him dealing with some who were to take advantage in an extremely negative way! This lad from a small Northern Valley Town was exploited and his kind and trusting nature was battered. His star rose high and fell down just as fast!

Strangers and hangers on in the art world won him over but hurt him badly! Those with a cruel streak and callous nature drove him to emotional turmoil! Even those who protected him. His family, agent and business advisors failed to prevent Mick snr's downfall!

Julie began to feel helpless! Watching her loving husband spiral out of control and fall into a world of booze, drugs and self-destruction! The temptations of the low life being one's he could not resist!

Eventually Julie brought Michael Jnr back home to England. To the safety of 'Steelsbridge'. A place where she was safe and could protect her son. Even though only ten year's old at the time Mick knew his mother had done exactly the right thing in returning home. His father had blindly become convinced that he was having the time of his young life!

Mick snr's short-lived life of fame was to diminish quickly! The once mild-mannered, sensitive and easy-going writer disappeared to be replaced by a personality full of spite and vindictive cruelty! Throwing the blame for his own failings at his family. Accusing Julie of running his life for her own ends and that his only lad Mick had been responsible for ruining their lives! He taunted them both for that long that the family was wrecked! All due to broken dream's! For Julie, the biggest blow came when she was accused of not allowing Mick Snr to be a free spirit as an artist and holding him back when young Michael had been born.

Mick's Dad became a violent man on his return home to Sheffield. Further drugs, drink and being drawn into petty crime led to some disgraceful behaviour! Not just in his home town of Steelsbridge but throughout Sheffield. Men he had grown up with all his life were astonished at the change in Michael Snr. Local's began to avoid any confrontation and abuse that they thought may be heading their way when the writer was half cut or paralytic! Which began to be a common occurrence! But the real heartache came along when he began to raise his fists to his wife and son. Young Michael and Julie were terrified! Emotional and physical damage left them both traumatised and having to deal with a legacy that looked impossible to heal!

In prison, Mick's old man mixed with hardened criminals! Quickly becoming a person to be feared and known to police as being big trouble! As a small town, Steelsbridge became notoriously linked with the once celebrated children's author!

Just before the Easter of 1958. In the late March of that year, Michael Snr met someone from his past! The family were having a holiday in London. For what became the end of an era for them all!

An American publishing agent by the name of Oscar Flint turned up in the Joyce's family life once more. Just like a really bad 'Yankee' penny or 'dime'! A man who had previously been a bad, if not to say, crazy influence on Mick Joyce Snr!

Flint turned up without warning! One night when Julie, Aimee and Michael had gone off to bed at the Starlight Hotel near Hyde Park in London. Flint had phoned Mick Snr and all his old reckless demons and wild behaviour resurfaced.

Oscar Flint had phoned the Hotel room number 1966 to tell Michael Snr some good news!

"Hi…Ya…Michael, man!" He had blurted out! "How the devil are 'ya'?" He added.

"Who is this?" Mick asked as his mind went into a state of flux at the sound of the strange, Southern American's droll.

"It's 'yar', old pal, Oscar, 'The Fixer' Flint man. Remember? How the devil are you, man?" Michael snr's heart suddenly sank to his boots! But then he began to feel warmer towards the caller as he recalled all the great times he'd experienced and all the good Oscar had once done for him! He had last seen this now 65-year-old agent in New York as Mick's book had been selling just like an American dream at the time! Back then the way in which Oscar Flint had looked out for his star writer was exciting and a breath of fresh air!

Oscar and Mick met in the lobby of the Starlight Hotel. They chatted over old times. Oscar then took his old friend into the West End. The beating heart of London. Mick had sneaked out of room 1966 while both Julie and Aimee slept soundly in each other's arms.

But Michael Joyce senior never did see his beautiful wife and child again after that night in London!

Oscar Flint hailed a black cab which then buzzed through London's hectic traffic. After visiting their old haunts of Soho and Camden. Oscar and Mick relived hedonistic days! Days of booze, uppers, downers and drugs! The days of women! But all this was far from fine. Mick snr's mind was broken! His thoughts became as black as that London night!

Michael William Joyce was found hanging by his pale white neck in Hyde Park in the early hours of Good Friday 1958! Just a few hundred yards from the Starlight Hotel on Lancaster Gate in West London. His young wife and small daughter, oblivious to their loved one's end, as they slept peacefully for the first time in months!

Mick's father was buried in the small graveyard of St Paul'sChurchin the quaint village of 'Smithsly', overlooking Steelsbridge – the Valley Town of his birth and where he had grown up. Mick's Dad had been born in Smithsly Village. The son of Jack and Phylis Joyce on their dairy farm on 24 March 1922.

Many famous folk flocked to the funeral. Actors, writers and artists came from all over the world to say a fond farewell to this accomplished author. Born with little but who became a local hero!

Little Aimee was far too young to be affected by her father's passing. But young Michael at just 18 was all too aware of the dark occasion! Standing by his father's coffin and taking a note from his pocket which was a poem. Father's favourite by Stevie Smith as the coffin was lowered gently into the deep open grave. The mourners all fell silent. With St Paul's behind them looking majestic in the bright Easter sunshine!

Young Michael read out 'Not Waving but Drowning'. Julie stood forlorn! Heartbroken and silent! She released a delicate yellow daffodil to float gently on the love of her life's coffin. The beautiful poem was then read and was also let go off from young Michael's grasp into his old man's grave!

That Easter Saturday of 1958 was so moving as a ripple of applause faded away! All friends, family and loved ones of Michael W Joyce saying their goodbyes!!!

Chapter 5

By the autumn of 1958 life was to get pretty much back to normal. Or as normal as Steelsbridge life could be!

Mick didn't mention his Dad's passing again. He took a train to Portsmouth following the funeral. Off he went back to sea. His silence being the way he chose to deal with the loss. But Mick was certainly affected by losing his father. More than he even realised as the year's passed by.

By this time my football career was going along very nicely. I was a regular in the Steels Town team. I had our manager Jack to thank. He showed great loyalty towards me. I was grateful for this and this help made me determined to keep on as first choice goalkeeper.

Life with Charlotte was also fine. All her work in getting through college had paid off! She then had combined a full-time position as a bank cashier with selling her art work at evening's and weekend's. Her passion for art won out when Miss Bailey, a former teacher who supported her, she also owned a shop in Sheffield. Tara Bailey's Art gallery and shop was just off the High Street next to the Catholic cathedral. This was where Charlotte and Tara became close friends. Then were later to come to an arrangement where Charlotte's art work was sold and a commission paid. This became a perfect understanding for them both.

In the February of 1959, the weather was foul! This being one of the worst winters ever seen in Steelsbridge. Deep snow along with below zero temperatures meant a freezing cold snap! This meant we couldn't train at the football club. Charlotte also along with everyone else missed many days at her work. Not being able to travel to the bank in Hillsborough. But the big thaw eventually came and spring blossomed in the Valley and we had a pleasant surprise!

Mick came home! His fortnight's leave coming on the back of his ship's return from South America. He had been to sea for 18 months. Telling us all this had been the most memorable of his Royal Navy service. He sat back in the 'Shakey' and polished off a few pints and whisky chasers before telling us.

"I've been to Brazil, Argentina and the Falklands this time, lad's…Oh Arr and 'lasses' … 'soz' Rach Charlotte, ha… Ha…ha… Good to be back in good old 'Shit Town'! I must say aho…aho…aho…" Our laughter enjoying Mick being in such high spirits lingered in the Tap Room air. Yes, Mick was on real good form back in the fold of home and his local. He was tanned as brown as the great 'Pele' of Brazil himself!

I could be guilty of drifting off in Mick's company at times. His leaves were familiar now and I thought he even began to bore himself once he'd knocked back a few Shakespeare beers and the rest. Not that I wasn't fascinated by his voyages around the world. But Rachel and Charlotte would always hang on his every word because they had never been abroad and Mick seemed to be able to broaden their horizons just by his recounting the adventures to foreign shores. I always veered to the bar to keep Frank company so leaving Mick with the girls.

"What's old Sam up to nowadays, kid?" Frank suddenly asked me.

"Oh, Sam's in Australia now, Frank. He's been over there a couple of years now man," I replied as I took a swift swig on my pint. "He plans to make 'OZ' his home, you know, Frank."

"Emigrate like?" I added calmly.

"Bloody hell!" Frank said spilling a dollop of his pint of bitter! Before drawing heavily on his cigarette.

"Thought I ain't seen him propping up my bar or down at "Old 'Ma' Palmer's Shop of Delights!" Frank had a wit and dry humour all of his own. All from all he had seen in the Valley over his time. A lifetime of drinking on one side of the bar or another of the 'Boozers' in the town! He had always struck me as a really easy-going bloke. But sometimes I saw him betray this a little. I'd often catch him with a real 'hang dog' look about him. On a break as he was leaning at the hatch of the Tap Room Bar, I did feel for him as you could have mistaken our landlord for having the world weighing on his broad shoulder's or with a dreamy, far-away look in his eyes! But that was nothing new in his pub. We were all guilty of this at times.

Frank stubbed out his fag and supped the rest of his pint.

"See you later, kid." Frank said eventually as he drifted back to his bar to continue serving folk. Feeling at a loose end I then went over to the notice board by the bar. There was never anything of note on there usually.Churchstuff and community goings on. Then I got a jolt to my system as a familiar and welcome voice had me turn around.

"Pint of the usual, Frank, please?" The customer asked. "Bloody hell fire…Blood…h…f…just been on 'bout thee'. Talk about that 'dam' devil and all that!" Frank's voice boomed out enough to wake them in hell itself!

I threw my arms around Sammy as I ran over to him! Almost knocking my old 'mukker' off his skinny legs and feet. I immediately noticed how much weight Sam had lost!

Not that he had ever been able to afford to do this! He looked absolutely exhausted! We ordered a tray of drinks for Mick, Rachel and Charlotte, who sat unaware that Sam was in. They were sat on over by the jukebox.

Frank kicked us out of the 'Shakey' in his usual friendly manner. Sam then invited us all back to his parent's place. They had a really lovely home. This was on the top road between Steelsbridge and Smithsly Village where Mick's Dad had been laid to rest.

Mr and Mrs Chivers or Amanda and Tony were fine folk with a pure heart of gold! OK for posh folk! I had once thought as a kid. Until I realised that people can be rotten and decent, whatever their class or wealth! Tony and Amanda had met at University in Oxford. He was born in Sheffield but Amanda had been born and bred in South London. Tony was a G.P at the local Valley doctor's surgery.

I always picked up a little on the thing that Sammy was a little embarrassed to have been born into an upper-class home. This may well have been my imagination but the privileged parent's situation and cut-glass accents were something I always did feel Sam wasn't altogether at ease with it?

His education and upbringing could only have been positive.

But still I always had the sense that Sam balanced his life between his folk's ways and him having always been great pals with myself, Mick, Charlotte and Rachel. He was very much aware of how raw and difficult our upbringing's had been! But never the less, Tony and Amanda were loving and proud of Sammy and his sister.

Wine and unique foods and snacks were always things I had always looked forward to when invited to Mr and Mrs Chiver's Cottage.

Charlotte was staggering a little as we left the Chiver's place.

"God, Gary, they are really 'sunmat', aren't they? Sam's Mum and Dad I mean. I was like I couldn't! I didn't want to put a foot wrong. It was so like…hic…hi…so bloody clean and neat and 'ti…' 't…' 'dy…' 'hic…'" She tried to say as she battled a bout of hiccups. We then tried to get across a farmer's muddy field from Sam's and make our way to Mrs Palmer's shop. We knew Mrs P would be open. She was open all hours. I wasn't too steady on me feet and Charlotte could hardly manage to put one foot in front of her other one!

By 6.00 a.m. in the morning, Charlotte pointed out a light in the distance. Mrs 'P's' front room window was like a welcoming beacon to us both!

"Come on, Gaz love, let's see if Mrs Palmer's home and see if she any fags to spare!"

"Oh, bloody hell, Charlotte! Do you have to? Do you have to fag it all time? Why can't you give 'em a miss for once!? I never could do with Charlotte and her smoking. I found her doing this a real 'drag'! Literally!"

"Oh, lighten up, Mr Minton, will you? M…Mrrr…bloody perfect all time." At this point I'd had enough of the day and went quiet on her. But still she insisted on picking a fight with me. She went on and on about how I'd never done anything risky or smoked or drank me 'sen' daft. She knew all too well that I needed to look after myself for the football. But when she was pissed like this, the silent treatment was always my best option. But this always brought out the worst in Charlotte. This was only a little spat. But the first of many!

Thank God Mrs Palmer was there to pacify us both! Tapping on her front door she beckoned us in.

"Come on in, you two." She called out from the kitchen.

Mrs 'P' was sat in her rocking chair. The coal fire's ember's burning out bright before her. Keeping the chill of the night away. Her beautiful black cat, Lucy, content on her lap.

"What's all this shouting all about, you two? You having a proper love birds tiff already, are you?" She smiled kindly at us both before removing her stunning red floral head scarf to reveal a tight perm of jet-black hair. No one I knew ever seemed to know of Mrs 'P's' actual age? Charlotte had once told me that while she was in care as a kid, she'd heard Mrs Palmer was in her 70's at that time. So some 15 years later she was indeed a grand old age! But the old lady was great! So young at heart and always so optimistic. Blessed with a cracking sense of humour and so caring.

We had sat in Mrs 'P's' kitchen that day as the dying embers of her coal fire faded away.

"Listen, you two." She had told us both before we left and Charlotte flicked away her tab end cigarette into the open coal fire as did Mrs Palmer.

"Life's too god damn short for bickering and playing silly beggars with one another. Come on now you two kiss and make up and stop being daft sods about it all!" she told us bluntly!

You could always rely on Mrs Palmer to tell it to you straight! As to if you took her common-sense advice was up to you. Of course. But Charlotte has always loved and respected her for this and so have I!

Chapter 6

By the morning of Christmas Eve 1960 I had decided to ask Charlotte something which was to petrify me.

Charlotte had just turned 20 years of age. I had celebrated my 20th on the 6th of August. A milestone I also shared with my good friend Frank our cordial, local landlord of the good old Shakespeare Tavern. So naturally we had a joint bash! Pity was that Sammy was unable to join us all though! He had been spending more and more of his time abroad as the years went by. We were all to see less and less of the lad in the Valley.

The Christmas tree in the 'Shakey' was decked out with splendour. Frank made a fuss of his customer's as always. It was the festive season again after all.

I took old Frank to one side just before folk flocked into the 'Shakey'.

"She loves the bloody bones of you, kid." Frank said to me!

"She will say 'yeah', don't you be worrying 'yeah sen' about that lad. If she 'dunt', she will have big old soft lad Fankie Taylor to answer to. I'm only kidding 'kidder' aha.

Don't thee fret. She will say 'yes'. Here, have free pint of this 'mucky shite' I 'alus' serve in here, Gaz."

Frank then placed an amber-coloured pint of his lager in front of me and we had a pint together.

That night was one of the best in the Valley for many year's. One which had cemented my friendship with Frank. We become real good mates.

Mick was pissed as usual! But he was still in great form. Even though he did go missing from around 10.00 p. m.. Mrs Palmer, Rachel and Charlotte had all been dancing together when Mick, not for the first time, stumbled and knocked the Christmas tree over! A drunken party trick he called this?

"Where's Mick, love? Do you know?" I asked trying to make light of things as well as work out which drink was mine from those covering the table. I had been pissed myself ever since that pint Frank had given to me on the house when he opened up.

"He was dancing with the 'Crimbo' tree just now, love!"

Charlotte replied, "That's the last time me and 'Rach' last seen him. But you know what was surreal, Gaz? You should have seen Mrs 'P' up and dancing with Mick while at the same time twirling Rachel around the "tree aha…ahaa."

We were all laughing at Mick and Mrs 'P's' antics that night!

"He only went and fell arse over tit!" Rachel then said trying to control her glee.

"Yeah…aha…ahaaa…! He eventually fell aha…amongst the baubles and decorations and then, oh…aha…then the bloody sparkly fairy falls from the top and hits Mick aha…aha…ahhha…! On the 'bonce'…oh…ahaaah…"

By midnight I had asked Charlotte back to Evie's. We were happy! When the cold night Valley air hit us outside. I sobered up with the thought of whether or not Charlotte would say yes or not?!

I let us both in with my spare key. The living room was dimly lit. The only light coming from a lamp with a bottle green shade and tassels. The room was chilly.

We didn't say a word to reach other at first. Both of us feeling the need to sober up from what had been a great night out! Sharing a comfortable silence. One which we were to share easily for many years to come.

Evie had been kind enough to leave a small buffet of food's and sweet's in the kitchen. Sandwiches', snack's, biscuits and some cakes Charlotte had made for us. She piling plates high with food. I was so nervous I made myself a cup of tea – sweetened with many spoons of sugar. We then eventually made small talk as we made ourselves comfortable on Evie's crimson sofa.

"Christmas will be over soon, Gaz. Far too soon. I'm really not looking forward to everything getting back to normal again." Charlotte remarked. Her voice weary and full of sadness after such a long day for us.

"I know love." I replied. "I always hate the matches at Steels between now and Easter time because the weather is always crap." I added.

I ended up babbling on quietly about how I'd like to maybe ask our manager Jack for a little more dosh in my wage packet? As well as maybe one day, maybe asking for a transfer to be able to further my career. But as I looked Charlotte's soft beautiful black hair trailed tenderly on to my shoulder's. A droplet of tears on her cheek with a trace of her mascara trailing from her tears. She was asleep.

When I woke up the room was freezing. Looking at my watch I realised that Sally would soon be waking up and be excited as she opened all her Christmas presents. So I then decided that if I didn't ask Charlotte at that very moment I never would!

Charlotte was now busy in the kitchen. The kettle boiling away. Sober. The cold hard reality of the morning had hit home. I was sweating a lot! My big goalkeeping hands were shaking. I knew I must ask her straight away!

The more I tried to think of how I was going to ask Charlotte, the more I became overwhelmed with confusion and panic! My head was spinning! My mind was racing fast. I just couldn't seem to calm my emotions.

Charlotte came to be with me from the kitchen. She placed my 'Steels' mug down before me.

"Christ, Gary. What the hell is eating away at you love? You're sweating, shaking and I don't know. What is it, love? Are you sickening for 'sumat'?" She then put her cold, tender, palm of her hand on to my temple. Her look of love and concern was something I didn't know how to take from her.

"Kind of," I said.

"How do you mean?" she muttered.

"Well,have…su…mat…to…a…as…k…you…Char…lo …tte?" I was a mess of nerves! Shacking again!

By the time Sally had raced into the living room to make light work of her presents, Charlotte had made my life a joy!

She knew all along what had been eating away at me!

"No, Gary. Please! Calm down. It's no big deal. I know exactly why you're in this state. Stop being daft, love."

She said, "Of course, I will bloody well marry you, you soft sod. Why wouldn't I?"

By the time Evie had made us all breakfast and 'Sal' had been oblivious to everything between her Uncle Gary and Charlotte – opening all her presents with such joy!

By that Christmas mid-morning, Evie opened a huge bottle of champagne she had been keeping on ice for such a special occasion! She had known from Frank at the pub all the time.

She had been tipped off by the big man about how I was to finally ask Charlotte to be my wife.

Between January and what was the glorious summer of 1961, both mine and Charlotte's lives were hectic. The arrangements for the big day kept us really busy. But the efforts we put in were well worth it! We had a fantastic day! The weather couldn't have been better and everything went off like a dream. On that July morning, Evie's flat had been given over to me. Oh, and my best man. Meanwhile Charlotte and her bridesmaid were preparing at her flat. Rachel lived with Charlotte back then anyway. They had both rented a ground floor flat across the road from the 'Steely WMC' on Valley Road. Rachel had been working at a factory in town. So with both their joint wage, they were well able to afford this – the rent and the bills.

"Where's me kecks, Gaz?" Mick asked as we both took over Evie's flat that morning.

"How should I bloody know?" I said as I struggled to sort out my Navy-blue tie in the mirror of Evie's bedroom.

"What are you like, you two…eh?" Evie said as she came in to her room, looking like a million dollars! Her golden fair hair hung down so natural over her turquoise trouser suit jacket. Her pale blue eyes were happy and proud. I was so emotional to have her with me and her to now not have to worry about her kid brother so much anymore.

About an hour later and in all her finery, Evie held on tight to a small bunch of yellow roses which I organised for her along with Mick.

By 2.00.p.m Mick was tapping again and again on the breast pocket of his Navy suit he had chosen to wear, which I was pleased about.

"Bloody hell fire, Mick, stop fretting about the ring. It's fine man. It's in there. Just give it over to me if you're worried," I said feeling tense and agitated about the day ahead.

"No, you're all right, Gaz. I just want everything to go off alright for you, pal. I don't want to leave 'out' to chance like."

St Pauls Catholic Church in the Idyllic Village of Smithsly was the setting for our big day. Mick nudged my right elbow as we stood waiting on the front pews of the Church as he sneaked a peek behind him.

"She looks like an angel kid." Mick whispered to me as all the guests shuffled about and rose to their feet behind us. I waited a while before finally sneaking a look myself. Charlotte looked divine. I tried to fight back the tears – tears of joy. She looked so lovely with her cream veil and simple white wedding dress with neatly cut jacket of ivory as a complement. Rachel then gently removed her veil as Charlotte's immaculate black hair fell gently down on to her shoulder's. Her chocolate brown eyes resembled those of a young child. All full of wonder and joy. With little make up she looked so natural and beautiful. I began to feel the luckiest man in the world to have found her.

Outside St Pauls the gentleman who had given Charlotte away also became the official photographer.

"Come on, Gary, Charlotte. Gary, give it 'thee' 'sens' under the wooden arch effort for this main photo." Frank Taylor was in his element. So proud was he to have given the lass away. To have been able to walk Charlotte down the aisle to be wed. Frank having never been married and never having been blessed with kids of his own. So he was so made-up. The photograph's he had taken were wonderful too. The one Frank had taken of us under the Church entrance archway hangs up in the pub. Having pride of place behind his bar. I have my Navy suit on. Pristine white shirt and lemon waist coat as Charlotte throws her yellow roses, bouquet above everyone's heads as the gentle shower of colours of confetti blew around us both as we laughed with joy together. It was as if the whole of Steelsbridge celebrated with us both in the 'Shakey' for the wedding reception. That's how I looked at things on the wedding night.

How great the pub had been decked out. Frank had taken away the snooker table which had dominated a third of the Tap Room. Replacing this with the D.J equipment. Sam had made a big effort to fly back from Australia for a fortnight in the Valley and since he loved his music so much he took care of the disco.

Lemon, Navy blue and white banners along with balloons had transformed Franks place. Along with Mick, Frank had also spent a week giving the walls, doors, ceilings and all the skirting boards a lick of paint. They had done both myself and Charlotte proud!

The highlight of our night came when Sammy chose two songs that meant the world to us both! Around midnight with balloons, banners and confetti being thrown up high in the Tap Room. Sam began to calm everyone down.

"I think you will all agree ladies and gents and you 'nippers', this has been a memorable day!" Sam said in such a refined way.

"We all know life can be hard here in the Valley and I'm always envious of those who make a success of their lives here. I just wish I could have found the right 'lass' to have made a go of things here myself!"

"Get on with it, you soppy sod." Mick called out before taking me by the arm and leading me up to the D.J set up. He then sandwiched himself between myself and Sammy. All three of us by this time looking unkempt, bleary eyed and worse for too much ale! Our neck ties had been thrown into a corner and our shirts were open and jackets tossed into the corners of the Tap Room. Our lemon waistcoats causing glee as they were all buttoned up in all the wrong places! Frank then made a dash from behind the bar!

"Say cheese again, please." Frank shouted out as he fumbled and laughed before taking another photo on this memorable day.

"These two songs are for my two lovely friend's. Two of the kindest folk I ever had the pleasure to know." Sam said as he wiped away a tear with the corner of his waistcoat.

Then once he had dimmed the disco lights, he threw a solitary white spotlight on myself and my new wife! Sam knew my all-time favourite song. Although I wasn't all that into music. Not in the way he was anyway but Otis Redding's *I've Been Loving You Too Long* had always been one I was really fond of. This was then blended neatly into Charlotte's choice of song.

We were holding each other close. Charlotte still perfectly dressed as when we had made our vows inChurchearlier that day. Her simple cream dress flowing elegantly around her feet. Her hair as fine and neat as at our 3.00 p.m. marriage In St Pauls.

Charlotte had a lot in common with Sammy where music was concerned. Having a large collection of vinyl records. One's she had collected since being a child in 'The Rose House' children's home.

My Baby Just Cares for Me by Nina Simon moved everyone. Some to tears. We both danced slowly in the spotlight. We were dancing as Gary and Charlotte Manners.

After the reception in the 'Shakey' we all helped in clearing up. But as we were doing so I noticed little Aimee Joyce, Mick's five-year-old sister slumped over on the seating which ran around the sides of the Tap Room. Julie had been helping Frank clear up. I raced over to them at once!

Chapter 7

Everyone was fantastic the night of our wedding in the 'Shakey'. Little Aimee was a very poorly five-year-old at the time.

Julie had picked her daughter up in her arms as soon as I had alerted her of the situation.

"Oh my God! Gary! She looks shocking!" Julie said, trembling and crying out for Frank to phone for an ambulance.

"Don't worry, Julie love. You carry Aimee to the beer garden seats outside. Get her some fresh air Frank. Quick! You phone the ambulance, mate, please!" I said as calmly as I could.

The ambulance was with us within minutes. Thank God! Julie and Mick then took little Aimee to the big Northern Royal Hospital on the north side of Sheffield! Speeding with sirens blaring through Hillsborough. An hour or so after being assessed at the Northern Aimee was taken to the Children's Hospital in Sheffield City centre. She was in expert hands there. The famous Sheffield Children's Hospital was the best and Aimee, we all knew would get the best of care there.

Mick and Julie were given their own room at the Children's by the doctors and nurses and told they could stay as long as they liked. Obviously both Julie and Mick were frantic with worry. But Mick's sense of humour could still lighten any crisis for everyone!

The next day was a very hot Sunday. That July day I came to the Children's with Charlotte. A Hospital well known throughout the country as the best! Situated near the University and across the road from the beauty of one of Sheffield's finest parks and gardens including the City museum.

"She's fine Gaz," Mick said as Charlotte and I entered the ward where Aimee had been brought in the previous night.

"She has just been running around in that big fancy park across road to buy herself an ice cream from Mr Softy's van. So I'm sorry, mate, you have both had a wasted journey." Mick's attempt at making light of things couldn't hide the fact he was in bits about Aimee. He hugged Charlotte and then shook me hard by the hand. The tears streaming from his reddened eyes!

"How's Julie?" Charlotte asked softly. Her kind voice helping Mick think more clearly.

Aimee was a very poorly kid for a while. That night of our wedding reception she had been rushed into intensive care. She was unconscious! The pain was intense to see her wired up to monitors and on drips and complicated Hospital equipment! Not even Michael and Julie were allowed into the intensive care ward but were able to have as much time as they needed to see through the window of the I.T Unit.

By my 21st birthday in the August of 1961, Frank, Sammy, Charlotte, Rachel and I had a chat in the pub on one of those weekend's before my big day. Frank made sure all his regulars had supped up and gone on their way home. He then put a cover over the snooker table so we could all sit around and talk.

Sam spent the rest of 1961 in Steelsbridge. He was so desperate to help out after what happened to little Aimee.

The Navy had been great and really understanding with Mick. Arranging for him to have generous periods of leave. Flitting between Portsmouth and Sheffield. They kindly gave him work in the shipyard in 'Pompey'. Right up until the beginnings of 1962.

As for both myself and Charlotte, we decided to take a well-earned break. Jack Burroughs at 'Steels' and Charlotte's work were kindness itself in giving us both time to recharge our lives.

When Aimee was finally discharged from the Children's she needed a lot of rest and care. Her recovery and convalescence at home was given expert guidance through Doctor Craig Brameld who was a fantastic support to the Joyce family.

In the August of 1961, our summer holiday began in the Shakespeare Tavern. Our genial local landlord Mr Frank Taylor hosted a special get together.

"Thanks a lot for coming along 'toneet' lad's and 'lasses'."

Frank said to us as he stood easily beside the old 'Shakey' snooker table. We all assembled on the stool's and chair's.

"You all know our Aimee has been 'right' poorly! Poor love. So I thought we would all try and help 'Doc Brameld' at the kid's Hospital and try make sure her little heart is so much better soon. Also to hope all the other little 'uns'…a…the…lad's and 'lasses' who are right poorly just li…like Aim…Aimeee get the 'right' good treatment."

"Bloody Hell!" Frank continued to say as he took a huge gulp of pint of muddy beer.

"Bloody Hell Fire!" Frank said out loud again as we could all feel he was losing the drift of what he had planned to say to us.

"I ain't said anything more than that in public in all my career in this 'Boozer'! Or anywhere else for that matter…God! I might have to sit me 'sen' down 'nah' and join you 'all'. We all at once shuffled about to make room for Frank to take a 'pew' after his speech.?

From then on that night, we all put our heads together and thought hard about how we could help our Aimee and the others in the Children's. We didn't take too long to decide what a difference we could all make!

The fortnight's break that year was taken up by Charlotte and us all, after that first meeting in the 'Shakey', working hard to organise and fund raise. A campaign which the Steelsbridge folk all got 100% behind. Doc Brameld was our inspiration to begin the fund raising with community events to take place and hopefully make such a huge difference to those poorly children whose hole in their hearts, just like Aimee needed so much love and care. Doctor Brameld had explained that a dozen or so kids had been admitted to the Children's. Ranging in age between babies and ten year's old.

All to intensive care! Children from Sheffield, Leeds and Nottingham between late August and the Christmas holidays of 1961, we were all to organise fun and games in the 'Shakey', as well as sponsored walks around the Valley and Hillsborough.

Then just before winter hit us a fantastic fun day on the pitch at 'Linden Park', home of Steelsbridge Town was arranged!

Chapter 8

Charlotte had never been to London before. Neither had I come to that. Neither of us had been any further than 'Skeggy' on our holidays in our lives. Her in all my 22 years and me because of all our concerns over Aimee during the last summer. Charlotte had thought it best if we put our honeymoon on hold until Aimee was out of the woods and stable and able then to have such a wonderful day at Linden Park. The day raising a couple of thousands of pounds for research into heart defects in folk of all ages.

The train left Sheffield Station early in the morning the week before Charlotte's 23rd birthday. A cold and frosty morning in late October. A Monday morning.

"Are you OK, Charlotte? You're quiet," I asked as the train pulled into Kings Cross, London.

"Yeah, I'm fine, love. I am just worried about what you told me." She said. I really began to fret then because I didn't have a clue what she was talking about. Then suddenly the penny dropped. I'd been having some problems at the club. I had been trying to weather the storm of having been dropped by the first team and for the past couple of months had kept this to myself! I had fallen out of love with the game. This had never been the case before and I couldn't handle how I was feeling. Jack had pulled me aside one day after training in pre-season.

"Can I have a word with 'ye', kid?" He had said calmly as he puffed away on one fag after another. Always a sign that all was not well with Jack! Or he had something important to say.

"Are 'ye' OK, kid?" Jack then asked me.

"Yeah, boss. I'm fine. Why? What's up?" I replied as I began to worry as to whether I had upset him or not.

"To be honest 'wi ye', kid, no. This situation 'wi' little Aimee seems to have took 'ye' mind off of 'ye' game, kid."

"Ye' did a grand thing 'wi' rest of town but I think it's effected 'yi' game, lad."

As soon as I got the nerve up, I managed to tell Charlotte that the gaffer had dropped me from the 'Steels' first team. I was still on the club's books but had to take a cut in wage as I was demoted to reserve team football. Charlotte had her secure job at the bank and extra income from producing her art work. So that was fine. Although I was determined to break back into the first team with 'Steels'.

"Oh, Gary, take no notice of me. I'm just 'witling' for now. Let's enjoy our honeymoon now. We can sort out all this money crap when we get back home."

We certainly did enjoy ourselve's too. We had an adventure and so much fun down in London. Charlotte had found a quaint little Hotel near to Hyde Park with all the smashing views with all the autumn colours and splendour. With all the trees fading caramel and brown hues.

The Hotel was only small with about a dozen rooms. A two-storey building decorated in 'Steels' club colours. Only a coincidence, of course. There was a bright blue front door with yellow porch canopy. The name 'Hyde Park Lodge' was set on a gold plaque on the wall above the main door with intricate black lettering.

"Oh, what a lovely room, Gary." Charlotte said as we placed our luggage on top of a spacious double bed.

"Yes it's 'oreight', Mrs." I said taking her hand as we stood at the window. An aged sash one which had an old sticker glued down in one corner.

"We will have that off!" I said laughing to myself.

"Gary! Don't be a soft lad. You will be having us kicked out before we have settled in." Charlotte then closed the heavy claret curtains, leaving the unpacking. We christened the 'Royal Hyde Park Lodge Hotel' bed for the remainder of our first night in that big, scary, beautiful London Town!

Back home in Steelsbridge both our jobs had been the cause of us feeling anxious and the fact that we didn't have a permanent home of our own was making Charlotte unhappy. She was still renting the flat across the road from the working men's club. A place Charlotte had lived with Rachel before we had begun courting. But this was far from ideal. I had still lived at Evie's. We really were desperate to buy our own property with Sally growing up. Room had become limited at my sisters. Although I was always more than welcome there, of course. But just before we had left for our honeymoon, Frank at the pub had suggested a solution for us that using the empty flat above the 'Shakey' might suit us.

So Charlotte's quiet mood on the way down to Kings Cross was all connected to these things. Money and our future living arrangements.

The first proper day of our honeymoon. The Tuesday was fantastic! Not! But the watery sunshine was pleasant. We had decided to cross the road from our Hotel by midday.

Charlotte looked really cute. Wearing a simple cream top and striking red jeans. We had both decided to wear trainers that day. She had swept her black hair back to her scalp and put this in a tight bun at the back. Tied with a delicate scarlet red ribbon. Charlotte never favoured make up. I was happy. We both were.

"I feel like a 'reight scruff! Charlotte!" I suddenly said as we walked hand in hand by the calming waters of the Serpentine in Hyde Park.

"I know, lad, 'tha' looks just like one." Charlotte said. Laughing out loud. She didn't usually have any particular accent when she spoke. But sometimes did the mock 'Stocky' or South Yorkshire one for a laugh. We both began to giggle like kids as I tossed a piece of crusty bread into the lake. Which landed with comic effect on the head of a solitary, passing duck.

"Good shot, Mr Minton!" Charlotte cried out!

"I bet 'tha' can't do that again." She added with glee!

"I can't, love. That's why I'm a crazy goalkeeper and 'nout' else," I replied.

For the rest of that Tuesday we were on bright, red London buses! Ones you were able to jump on and off by way of the back. These being the famous 'Route Masters'. Unlike the buses in Sheffield where we paid a conductor once the driver's door opened at the front. We jumped off and on just like 'giddy' school kids. We stood holding on to the rail at the back. Then the 'clippy' or conductor bloke let us have his coal black cap with 'London Transport' emblazoned on there. With a shiny big badge of red and gold. Charlotte and I taking it turns to welcome passengers aboard. She would laugh out especially if a Londoner got on our bus. One elderly gent said to us, "What's 'geein' on here? Ah, well, makes a nice change misery 'guts' 'chippy's' we usually get here 'darlings'!"

I went upstairs after a while because these were open top 'Route Masters'. I was amazed at how you could chop off the roof of a double decker bus! I think the sunshine and our High Holiday mood brought out all the fun in us both. We got some curious and puzzling looks on those buses that day from Londoner's. We buzzed all around that wonderful Capital City. We also explored our way around by the remarkable black carriage cabs and the unreal subway. The famous London underground!!! Charlotte was a little unnerved by life down there. I wasn't comfortable deep down there either. Under the earth, I began to feel claustrophobic and unable to handle all the hustle and bustle of folk jumping on and off those tube train things.

We both adored the sights of Buckingham Palace, Harrods and Trafalgar Square.

"Don't bloody be daft, Gary. You young idiot." Charlotte called out to me in Trafalgar Square as the blistering hot sunshine delighted everyone. The tourists, local's and workers who were seeming to be skiving from their City and various places of work. From shops, restaurants, bars or wherever of the Capital.

"I'll be 'Oreight', Charlotte. It's not that high up here. I am a Leo after all, love!"

That photograph Charlotte took of me on top of one of the majestic black lions that sit proudly at each corner of Nelson's Column is one of our real favourites. The photo now sitting proudly on top of the television at our Evie's flat. I am wearing the bus conductors black, red and gold cap which he so kindly gifted us as a lovely souvenir, memento. The conductor was called Otis and he had made a brand-new life for himself in London. One of many who had done so by travelling from abroad to the greatest City of this world of ours.

During our honeymoon fortnight we had a variety of experiences. Mixing our days between taking a leisurely stroll through the Royal Parks. Charlotte was in awe of St James's Park in particular and of Regents Park too. But we were forever drawn back to our digs near Hyde Park by the close of each day. Building up a close friendship with Mr and Mrs Omalley who ran our Hotel. Mrs Omalley insisted we call them both by their first names. Her husband Jim said the same.

"OK then Mary," Charlotte had said. "Well, I'm Charlotte and this is my 'gormless hubby', Gary!" She added with nerves showing in her speech. She had always back home in Steelsbridge been in the habit of breaking the ice with folk in introducing me in this way.

Mary and Jim suddenly looked blank at each other? Puzzled and unsure of what Charlotte had meant. Mary was small in stature with stark, orange hair. She had the palest of blue eyes that were so intense and striking. Mary had on a dazzling emerald green pinny, which was a real sign she was so proud of her Irish homeland. Jim on the other hand was tall and as skinny as a drainpipe. He was well over 6" tall and had a striking Teddy boy quiff which was swept over his balding scalp. His jet-black hair plastered down with brylcreem. His white discoloured shirt having seen many a better day. The material of his Grandad shirts all worn out and tired. All the time Jim had a fag end, one of his roll ups dangling, un-lit from his lips. His angular jaw not having seen a razor in a long time. There was always a betting slip hanging out of Jim's shirt pocket. His shoes were the ones fashionable during the 1960s. Literally the Blue Suede shoes of that particular era.

Jim and Mary looked at each other and then burst out laughing.

"Gormless!" They both cried out as one.

"What in heaven's name is 'Gormeyless'?" Jim said as he took a seat at the little bar in the Hotel. He then began to chuckle to himself on and off for the remainder of our stay all about this!

Every time the Omalley's saw us, they would both say,

"Hey, we're both 'gormless' today, Mr and Mrs M." taking to addressing us in this way as Mr and Mrs 'M'.

Mary and Jim asked us out one day. They were going off to the seaside of Brighton. We were both moved by their offer and so chose to get off their. They had both been running another Bed and Breakfast Hotel on the seafront in Brighton. This was more of a place they intended retiring to really. Where they would eventually make a home and invite friends and family from over the water in Belfast to stay with them.

Charlotte wasn't too keen on Brighton. The Omalley's were understanding and on the Sunday morning on the day before Charlotte's 23rd birthday we all came on back to the Hyde Park Lodge in London.

On Bonfire Night of 1961 Charlotte woke up before me. Catching up on her sleep until the time came for us to go down for breakfast by 9.00 a.m. She chose to wear a bright red t-shirt which depicted scenes of London with gold and silver markings. James and Mary had a surprise for Charlotte. Placing a delightful birthday cake on the breakfast table amongst the boiled eggs, toast, marmalade and tea pots.

"Oh, 'Wow'! How did you both know?" She asked. The emotion of the big day beginning to take her over. We then all sat around at this table.

"A Yorkshire 'birdy' told us, sweetheart." Mary said smiling kindly at Charlotte. Jim then struck up a match to light the simple golden candle that sat proudly within the cake's icing.

"Oh thank you Gary love. That is so very sweet of you!" Charlotte said as we then all began to sing Happy Birthday to her. We then all began to relax for a while.

The Hyde Park Lodge had a simple set up. The rooms arranged with easy access. Once through the main doors from the street outside, you would confirm your booking at reception. With a neat array of room keys arranged on hooks. A quaint silver bell on the desk was there to alert the Omalley's if they were otherwise engaged in running the Hotel. The dining room was at the back of the building. This doubled up as the bar and breakfast dining room as well as for evening meals. A room nicely decorated a shade of light green and cream, complemented by picture rails, doors and the sash windows as well as the skirting boards with ivory gloss paint. Set into the feature wall was an open fire place with red and emerald green tiles placed perfectly around the fire. A long, fine burgundy Chesterfield sofa occupied one corner of the living room, come dining room. A black and white television set with doors of dark oak which closed up when the TV was not in use. A large mirror on the wall above the fireplace was a lovely touch and a couple of pretty ornament's sat on top of a television cabinet. These were comical little Irish leprechauns with hat's jauntily falling off their heads.

"Ah, I can see you are both amused at Mary and James 2 Gary." Jim said as we sat sipping our cups of tea that morning.

"How do you mean, Jim?" I asked feeling confused.

"The two leprechauns 'lad' on top of our TV set there. There our pride and joy are, they not now, Mary girl?" Jim spoke with such pride smiling and winking to Mary as he spoke.

"Oh, 'Yeah', sorry." I ended up saying. "They are really great." I added. Not really getting the passion old Jim had for his little Irish ornament friends.

"They are always pissed off." Mary Omalley said then and we all four of us were hysterical with laughing. Mary we found had a wicked, blunt sense of humour about her.

"Jim, Gary was curious to know all about the sticker in the corner of the window of our room." Charlotte said later that morning.

"Sticker, love? What sticker is this?" Jim asked with a puzzled expression. But then changed to nod at Mary with a mischievous glint in his eyes.

"Ah yes, young Sheffield people." James remarked.

"Well, when I was just a young man, I would have been around your age, young Mr Gary. I supported the Chelsea for my many sins. When I came here from Belfast to look for some work to help Mary and feed our kids back then I made pals with a couple of lad's from the Kings Road.

"The Kings Road, Jim?" Charlotte then asked.

"Yes, dear, that's in Chelsea, where all the posh folks hang out and live. Those West London lot." Jim explained.

"Oh, 'Yeah', I see. Of course." Charlotte replied quietly.

"Well, I got some work as a painter and decorator and these two lad's lived only a stone's throw from Stamford

Bridge – the Chelsea football ground." Jim said as he enjoyed reliving the time in his life when he was young and pretty much carefree!

"So," he continued to say to us.

"They used to let me have ticket's at half price for the Chelsea home games." Jim said.

Then suddenly Mary jumped up and knocked over her cup of tea! Dropping her half-smoked cigarette as well.

"That's 'alus' happening to me and 'Jimbo'." Mary said with a hint of panic. They then leapt over to save one of the leprechaun ornaments which had come crashing down on to the floor!

"Good catch, girl!" Jim then cried out. Laughing and then throwing his own tab end cigarette with some joy into the waste paper bin.

"She'd make a fine fielder at the old Lords cricket ground so she would folks." Jim then cried out with such fun before falling back into the comfort of the Chesterfield settee.

"So where the devil was I? Oh yeah! I started to get hooked on watching the Chelsea. I still go from time to time now when the crowd is not so hectic if you get what I mean?"

Jim said as he turned to Charlotte and I listened intently too!

"Do 'youse' follow the football, Mr and Mrs 'M'?"

He asked with respect.

"Oh yeah." Charlotte replied happily.

"Well, not me so much but Gary plays for our local team. He's their first-choice goalkeeper. He's quite a talent so I've heard Jim, is my other half." The joy in Charlotte saying this of me was really pleasing. I couldn't help but blush.

"Ah, Charlotte love your making the lad colour up there just like a 'wee' child so you are." Mary said as she rose from her chair to give me a tender hug.

"Oh wow, young Gary. Tell us more. I love my football. Who is this dynamic team you play in goal for, lad?" Jim asked me.

Mary and Charlotte cleared up all the cups and saucers and then went for a chat in the kitchen. Leaving me with Jim to then discuss the 'beautiful game'. Something both Mary and Charlotte had in common. I was to discover during our stay was they didn't have the slightest interest in football. Or did they didn't understand the game much either.

The 'Hyde Park Lodge Hotel' was quiet as far as having guests staying was concerned during our honeymoon week there. So the Omalley's then suggested we all go out. They took us to some of their old haunts of the Capital. Some of the most famous of sights. Sights they had loved when they first made a new life in London Town about a decade before.

James and Mary had an old turquoise Morris Minor. They had tooted around all over in from time to time over the year's. There was more rust than actual bodywork holding the thing together though. The seats were ripped and torn and there was the odd spring jittering from the upholstery!

"How would you like to go down by the 'mucky' river which local's call 'The Thames' you two in this old 'Morris'?"

'Morris' Jim's little car could be seen for the rest of our honeymoon holiday struggling around the historic London sights. Charlotte sat cramped in the back seat with Mary while I tried to read a battered old London map to try and help Jim negotiate the heart of the City.

"I've lived here for year's Gary, my man. But you ask me where anywhere is and I am 'banjaxed!', son." Jim said as he constantly puffed away on his roll up. I just had to laugh as we made our way across Westminster Bridge. Old 'Morris' was making an horrendous racket! This motor had already had her life and every now and again a loud bang and a black thrust of smoke from her exhaust brought attention from all who were passing by on the bridge!

"Oh, don't worry about old 'Morris', everyone. She gets all grumpy whenever she has to go amongst the busy London folk and she has to kick out a bit of the old exhaust dust! It's just her showing off 'aha!'. She's a real old character!"

During the final week of our honeymoon we took loads of photographs of Big Ben and the Houses of Parliament! of Tower Bridge and the Tower of London. We limped in old 'Morris' down Oxford Street where Mary and Charlotte spent up! Buying all the delights those shops sold!

Meanwhile, I went with Jim to a couple of pubs he knew well in the West End in Piccadilly and Soho. We chatted at length about football. But once we had 'supped', more than our fair share of the old Guinness I became far too maudlin. Opening my heart to him all about 'Steelsbridge.' Of how the fulking place had provoked all my anger sometimes! Of my worries for our Evie and Sally, of course. I began to go on too much all about Sammy and Mick and so much more I had bitter issues with about that bloody Valley!

As were sitting in a cosy little old London Tavern close by Soho Square, I then was taken aback to learn that Jim had a calm and reflective side to him. Ever since we had arrived at their digs on that Monday all myself Charlotte had known of James and Mary Omalley was that they seemed fun and kind hearted. But as we sat outside the 'Laughing Man' by the Square, Jim's mood began to alter. I think mine did too. The Guinness had brought out far too much of the melancholy within the both of us.

"I'll give 'ya' bit of my daft old wisdom, young Gary, my friend." James said as we sat outside that 'Laughing Man' Boozer in Soho and the place became deserted.

"You don't worry about everyone else, lad. If you can live a truthful life thru…tru…" Jim then had a fit of the hiccups as he tried in vain to empty the last of his pint of dark bitter tasting Guinness.

"Truthful." I said as I also found myself slurring my words as some rare November sunshine and the alcohol took effect on us both.

Chapter 9

Our train was due to leave Kings Cross Railway Station at 5.00 p.m. on the Sunday evening. Our fantastic honeymoon had sped by so quickly. Because we had little clean clothing left before boarding the train home. Charlotte and I had nipped off to a local London market just near our Hotel to buy 'clobber' for the journey back to Sheffield. Charlotte chose a simple white plain blouse and comfortable trousers of Navy blue and wore her red slip on – ballet type shoes. I chose to wear a football shirt. One in claret and blue. These were the colours of West Ham United. I didn't wear this with any loyalty to this club. I just needed something to travel in. Otherwise, I wore some black jeans and simple slip-on shoes. Charlotte was looking tired. Her dark hair falling in tiny whispering trails. Her eyes bleary. Her face pallid. I could feel all the past days catching up on me too. looking in the Hotel mirror before our train left for home, I was backing away quickly after noticing the black circles beneath my eyes from the lack of rest and lack of sleep.

Jim and Mary Omalley helped us to platform 9 of Kings Cross Station. We were all quiet. Not really in a mood for conversation. Sad to be having to say goodbye to each other after a fine time.

We fell to sleep as soon as we had settled in our seats on the train. The autumn weather in London as we left had been just fine. Not so hot as to be uncomfortable but not too chilly either. This was the climate as we came away from London that November day.

We were nudged awake as we came slowly into Sheffield Railway Station just shy of 9.00 p.m. that Sunday night.

"Come on, you two love birds, get 'thee sens' up and lively. You are back in Sheffield now." The guard was kind. Despite his brusque manner. He then nudged another couple in a seat nearby to wake up and then I helped Charlotte with the luggage. Taking our cases down from the overhead rack above. We then jumped from the train on to the platform.

The cold, bitter air hit us both. Clearing our sleepy heads. There was a light drizzle and a weird kind of misty look about the place as we came out of the Station concourse. Charlotte took out her big black overcoat from one of the cases and I put on my duffle coat. We then walked out into Sheffield and received a lovely surprise!

My short cropped blonde hair stood up on end. The constant drizzle soaking me through. I then caught sight of a very weary looking man! The large glass windows surrounding Sheffield Station by the main doors reflected my weary and dishevelled state. What I noticed with real unease was the way my pale blue eyes stared with a faraway lost and deep loneliness.

"Oh, wow, what a lovely surprise!" Charlotte cried out and this was when my sorrowful mood lifted. There by the small Station café was little Aimee holding hands with her Mum, Julie, who then ran on over to embrace us. Aimee then threw her arms around Charlotte's legs. The drizzle rains then began to ease and then suddenly stop. The cold night air then became milder and Julie told us fantastic news as we then travelled back to Steelsbridge in a black taxi cab.

"She's been given a clean bill of health Charlotte. Gary, God, I'm so relieved. What a weight off now I am able to tell you both!" Julie then hugged Aimee close to her as they sat in the back of the cab on the way home. Aimee then played in wonder with my still damp and spiky blonde hair. I kept shaking my head as playful puppies sometimes do when they have been frolicking in the rain.

"Oh, wow! That's wonderful news! Aimee looks so well now. You must come over to mine and Gary's house warming when we have something to warm up that is aha…aha!" Charlotte said smiling broadly and trying to forget all her own weariness of the past couple of weeks and our journey home from London. Aimee giggled most of the way home to the 'Valley!'.

"Oh, you're so funny, Aunty Charlotte." Aimee said quietly as she then kissed her gently on the mouth. Before taking hold of her Mum's hand and they both skipped on into the house!

Once we had arrived back at Evie's on the Foxley Estate, Charlotte suddenly began to weep! We asked Evie if she didn't mind if both myself and Charlotte could stay with her now we had returned from our honeymoon. Our favourite place had always been Evie's. All due to doing our courting there. The living room in particular being such a fondly remembered place. But every day since that Christmas time the five years before I had been in a kind of 'flux'. Those five year's had simply sped by and we had been so happy! My having to console my wife now after her getting so fond of Aimee had brought on some turmoil for me!

Just after midnight, Charlotte chose to leave Evie's, going back to the Valley Road flat. I was worried since our wedding day I had learnt more about her and especially more about myself. I was baffled sometimes!

"Don't worry, Gary, I will be fine. Rachel will be back in the morning and you have to start back training, don't you? Tomorrow, I mean?" When Charlotte began sobbing I was at a loss as to what to do really? I glanced at my watch as we both stood in silence on Evie's doorstep. I was desperate for Charlotte not to walk the whole way across Steelsbridge. To walk across the town at such a late hour on her own.

"I will phone you when I get home, love. I love you so much, Gary!" she said as her tears still dried and her black hair trailed over her face. Her bright, kind, black eyes were so deeply sad though.

"I'm so sorry about earlier tonight Gary." Charlotte said some half an hour later. Having walked past Flora Palmer's shop and the Shakespeare pub and then the posh Donley housing estate and eventually arriving home at the 'Steely' club flat by way of the well-lit 'gennel.' Which is a short cut off the Donley estate. The flat overlooked the 'Steely W.M.C' within a block of eight flats.

I returned to training with 'Steels' the next day, a Monday morning. All the lads were great with me. There was the usual banter and 'mucking' around.

"Good of 'ye' to join us at long last, lad. How long 'wee' that honeymoon? Seasons all but over kid." Jack Burroughs called out in his usual darkly funny way as we all assembled in the centre circle at Linden Park Stadium.

"Welcome back 'laddy!'" He then remarked clapping his hands and then making us all listen up!

"Ney, then, lad's. It's those 'Geordy' boys. Sunderland coming here Saturday." As some of the lads were still not paying attention and displaying some horse play and loud chatter. Jack began to raise his voice to us all.

"Ney! Come on, 'ye' idle sods. Come on now, shut 'yer' racket and listen on up." Jack was serious and we all knew this now. He had kidded us long enough and silence fell over Linden Park. We then knew we needed to get our heads down and train hard for the match on Saturday against Sunderland.

I was so relieved when the training session ended as Jack was waiting to usher the rest of the lad's off home after we had showered. But I couldn't shoot off for the afternoon straight away! The gaffer wanted a word in his office. A small place which was up the stairs above the dressing rooms and both tea and licensed bars. Jack would very rarely see me or anyone else in there at the Linden Park Stadium.

I was not looking forward to this to say the very least! Not after the last conversation I'd had with Jack Burroughs prior to us leaving for London for the honeymoon. I hadn't showered or changed. I still wore my emerald green keeper's jersey and 'Steels' gold shorts and socks. My cotton green gloves trailing in my right hand. My heavy boots resounded out as I took each step up the metal stairs. The office door was wide open. A simple yet faded gold plaque with white letters on that door read 'MANAGER'!

Jack Burroughs was always one for wearing a pin striped black suit. He was small of stature. Broad and heavy set. He had jet black, slicked back hair. Always well-oiled to his scalp. A life weary look about him. Jack was marked by crow's feet. His eyes a mixture of browny-green. These were kindly eyes unless someone happened to cross him. Then there would be a quick blaze of anger before settling down to his mellow kindness again.

I knocked lightly on the gaffer's door.

"Come on in, lad. 'Ye' looking fit and well. Had a good time 'ye' two down in that mad smoky London did 'yer'?" Jack asked me as he stood holding out his hand which I shook firmly!

"Yes, boss, thanks. It 'wa' great! We both really enjoyed ourselves, thanks," I said as I took the seat Jack had offered to me.

"Good, lad. Do 'ye' know why I've asked 'ye' up to me 'Ivory Tower'? 'Ney' don't bother to answer that kid. How would 'ye' know anyway? Don't fret though. It's good news for 'ye', kid…relax, Gary lad," Jack said.

I then relaxed back into the chair.

I could have flown down those iron steps from the gaffer's office. My heart light as I'd could ever remember! The rush of adrenalin through my veins was euphoric! I couldn't wait to see Charlotte and tell her my wonderful news!!!

I was pleased but settled for phoning Charlotte later in the end. She was exhausted! The bank had been a lot busier than usual before we had left for London on our honeymoon. She had also spent a lot of her spare time then helping me out.

"Charlotte! The gaffer has told me I'm gonna be a permanent until the end of this season. I'm going to be back in the first team, love. Back on my usual pay, wages!"

"Oh, that's fantastic news, Gary! I'm so pleased. Jack's always liked you. He's treat you like really well always. Hasn't he?" She said with so much life and enthusiasm. So I think this was just as great news for me as Charlotte. The brightness had returned to our lives. I could sense even talking to her over the phone that her mood was positive again.

The following weekend Charlotte just wanted to have a quiet Sunday night over at the pub. The 'Shakey' was pretty much deserted. So, Mrs 'P', myself, Charlotte and Big Frank settled down for a friendly game of cards.

"How did 'tha' get on 'wi' those foreigner's 'int' London Town then?" Frank asked. His wry, mischievous smile came as he pretended to study his hand of cards.

"Pontoon you Losers!" Frank hollered out as he licked his fore finger before placing the red heart of diamonds on his other cards on the table before him!

"What foreigners, Frank?" How do you mean, love?"

"Londoner's Charlotte. Bloody Southern softies." Frank replied as we all laughed at old Frank's take on where we had been for the past couple of weeks.

"Mrs P…Mrs P…It's your move, love," Frank said as he put his playing cards away out of sight. The 'Shakey' was so quiet this night. We were at a table close to the bar in the Tap Room! But Frank only had the one customer to serve all night.

"Less of the 'love', Frankie Taylor. You will get no cuddle at closing time! Cheeky young devil." Mrs Palmer told our landlord as she winked at him. The big man then drew out his huge white handkerchief from his trouser pocket and chose to wave this high above his head. Before wiping away an imaginary tear from his eyes with the 'hanky!'.

As we waved our goodbyes to 'Big Frank', Charlotte made sure that Flora got back home safe and sound to the shop.

"I'm just seeing Flora home, love. Put the kettle on and don't eat all those 'sarnies' Frank let us have." Charlotte said to me.

Time sped on by! Charlotte was becoming unhappy working at the bank. But since that quiet yet enjoyable night with Flora and Frank at his pub she had received an offer.

With Charlotte's time becoming precious in the run up to Christmas she told me about the change. She had been working all week at the bank and all her weekend's too at Tara's shop. Tara had been looking to expand and had asked Charlotte to be involved.

I'd thought Tara's offer to Charlotte of opening another Art Shop made perfect sense. Not that I knew all that much about business. But the shop on the High Street in town had been selling both Tara's and Charlotte's work and attracting other talented artist's, whose work had been bringing in valuable commissions for the girls.

"This just feels right, Gary, to leave the bank now." Charlotte said to me at her Steels Road flat over a 'cuppa'.

I agreed with Charlotte about the idea for Tara to open another Art Shop in the Hillsborough area of Sheffield. This made perfect sense. They were both experienced enough to make a success of things! But I wasn't without my concerns about the venture. Charlotte being in charge of the new Hillsborough shop would be a gamble. Where as if she stayed with the bank she would still bring in a regular wage.

But Tara had the funding to start up 'Tara's Art.' The name chosen for the new shop that Charlotte would have sole charge of running. She was so delighted with the faith her good friend had shown in her.

Chapter 10

The halcyon days of my life with Charlotte came as 1962 dawned. Reaching their glorious end in the summer of 1966!

Mick and Sammy began to seem more like strangers as time sped on by. Mick's Naval days fading away by the time he was 26. Sam hadn't been back to the Valley since Aimee had fallen ill. By 1965 he had gone back to London, deciding he was going to live a simple life there. His labours in Australia not being able to satisfy him. So he had bought a studio flat on the embankment close to the River Thames. Deciding to pursue a career as a freelance writer. Something his parent's approved of and an ambition he had always secretly yearned for. So this was to become a full-time endeavour and labour of love for the lad.

What at first had seemed a big risk for Charlotte to leave her job at the bank would eventually work out very nicely! Money had always been limited for us. But by 1962 our lives had begun to blossom in this way. I commanded a regular place in 'The Steels' team, which would last for the next four seasons in which I broke a previous club record for keeping clean sheets.

The season of 1963/64 was a particular highlight. Jack Burroughs's had promised to deliver a trophy for Steelsbridge Town ever since he had arrived at the club. He was well aware how much the board and Chairman of the club craved success.

They were patient with Jack and this was something which eventually paid off. In the 5th season of Jack's management of Steels, a trophy was ours! A major honour in the form of the League Cup. The club's first significant silverware since they were formed in 1946.

The League Cup had only been competed for since 1960. Each round was played over two legs and the winning team were those who won out on aggregate. We had breezed through the rounds and even beaten a well fancied Liverpool in the Semi Finals. So Jack expected this form to continue in the final and was disgusted when 'Steels' lost 2:0 to Leeds Town. The gaffer was furious with us all! I held my hands up as I could have done so much better with both of the goals we conceded. Jack kept us in the away team's dressing room at Elland Park that night and gave us hell!

"'Ye Canny' just turn up and think 'ye' have already BLOODY won this Cup! 'Yeee' know!!!" He had bawled out for all the ground to hear. Before ending up telling us to get our act together even more!

"I'M TELLING 'YEE' ALL NOW 'YE' WERE ALL OF 'YE' ABSOLUTE SHITE! I'VE 'ALUS' DRILLED IT INTO 'YEES' THAT 'YE' SHOULD RESPECT EVERY DAMN TEAM WE PLAY 'NAY' MATTER WHO THEY ARE. BE IT A NON-LEAGUE OUTFIT OR CHAMPIONS 'O' EUROPE!!!"

Any attempt by us all to object or dispute anything Jack Burroughs had to say to us at the end of that Leeds first leg was swiftly quashed. We all knew we had not done our best.

I was low. I took our manager's harsh yet understandable words very much to heart. I had forgotten the basics of goalkeeping and I was determined to redeem myself!

The second leg of the League Cup Final back at Linden Park was a totally different story. Linden Park had always been without floodlights. Something which Jack Burroughs had been in discussion with many times over the years as manager. So because of this situation the 'Steels' v Leeds Town second leg took place on a Thursday afternoon. The match was one in which we made a nervous start. With Jack's words still hanging over us all and showing Leeds far too much respect. But once I had made a decent save as a Leeds player hit a fine shot low to my right, which was heading for the goal, we improved. A couple of minutes later I kicked the ball out of my hands high and long to the edge of the Leeds penalty area. Our centre forward Dave King headed the ball down into the stride of midfielder Max Scott to score with a rocket of a shot into the roof of the goals! This lifted us and confidence grew. Scott scored again from the penalty spot in the second half. We could see as we waited to kick off the 30 minutes of extra time that Leeds Town were spent!

With just five minutes left to play we scored from a corner giving Max Scott his hat trick and man of the match and Steelsbridge Town their first major trophy! Because we had a league match at home on the Saturday, celebrations for our first cup win were put on hold. But the next day Jack Burroughs and everyone who worked so hard at 'Steels' partied in the 'Shakey!' Big Frank doing us all proud once again in organising the 'bash'!

1962 was a memorable year! We were invited back down to London. Charlotte had received a phone call one evening from Mary Omalley inviting us both back to the 'Hyde Park Lodge'. This was a wonderful time. Our honeymoon the previous year had been brilliant and we looked forward to returning to renew our special friendship with Jim and Mary.

But by the autumn of 1964, our visits to stay with the Omalley's changed. Jim had been feeling fragile ever since the spring time of 1963. He had been suffering with chest pains and had fallen ill a few times. Mary and Charlotte spoke to me a lot. Asking my advice as to if the best thing to do was to possibly sell the Hyde Park Lodge Hotel and finally retire to their Brighton home? So when we did go back to London again Jim was relieved to agree with me that the 'Lodge Hotel' had probably become too much for himself and Mary and retirement to the Brighton Coast was for the best.

An exciting time came along for Charlotte just after she had celebrated her 25th birthday. Thanks to Flora Palmer at her shop – Charlotte's life and work flourished!

"Hello, you two. Is everything going well?" Flora had asked once she had put boiling water over some loose tea in her favourite bright red tea pot as Charlotte sat nursing Lucy. Mrs Palmers beautiful black cat.

"How is everything, Flora?" I then asked

"Oh, you know, Gary lad. Can't grumble. Apart from the old age and poverty of course aha! Oh, and the not taking any notice of what folks say of me in this strange old town aha!" Flora remarked, drawing heavily on a cigarette while she still chuckled away! But the guttural sound of Mrs 'P's laughter made me think she should maybe cut down some on the old 'Park Drive's Ciggies'!

As we walked home that day from the shop, Charlotte mentioned something that I too had noticed about Flora.

"Something's definitely up, Gary." Charlotte said to me as she put her hand through my arm which I then snuggled into my jacket pocket.

"I know love." I replied. "Flora hasn't been herself for quite a while now, has she?" The fact we had now been married for a few year's helped, I sensed that Charlotte had concerns about folk we both loved and cared for. Friends and neighbours without wanting to intrude would visit Flora at the shop once we slowly got the word around that we were concerned for Mrs P's welfare. Charlotte helped out in her shop more and I did the same.

By the time we had all celebrated our League Cup Final success in the spring of 1964 Charlotte was jubilant too. After a lot of advice and discussion amongst folk, who thought a lot of Flora Palmer in the Valley. Our dear friend made a decision to move on. Flora had been born in the house where she now owned her shop. She had been away to London and elsewhere in her life but all any of us younger folk could remember was the old 'lass' living at No 1 Steel Road in the Valley town of Steelsbridge. Flora had not made use of the upstairs bedroom's for many a long year now. She had been unable to climb her stairs due to infirmity and lived in the kitchen at the back of her shop. The kitchen and bathroom was downstairs anyway in these old properties. The kitchen was vast so Flora had plenty of room for her single bed. An open fire in there made life very cosy for both her and 'Lucy'.

After a lot of arranging and conversation it was decided that Charlotte would buy the old place from Flora. The dear old lady comforted by knowing my wife would take good care of the place. So by the winter months of 1964 Charlotte moved into No 1 Steel Road and made plans to convert the place into an Art Gallery and coffee shop and then live in the upstairs rooms. Converting the box bedroom into a bathroom and toilet.

"I'll be sad to leave here, love! But I'm glad I will be leaving the old place in such good hands. You have both been so grand about all this." Flora told both myself and Charlotte in the kitchen of Steel Road that everything she owned had been put in the removal's van. Frank from the pub had managed to acquire a nice big removal wagon. Mrs P was tearful but also cheerful about making a new life for herself. In fact Charlotte and Rachel were more emotional!

"Bloody hell fire!" Mrs Palmer shouted out as she locked up the old shop for the very last time!

"You'd have thought that someone had popped their clogs. I'm only moving a few streets up Valley. Come on, you two. Onwards and Upwards to 'Sweetly House'." Flora looked amazed as she said this at both Rachel and Charlotte both dabbing away salty tears from their faces. But Mrs 'P's' laughter became infectious and we all ended up joining her in breaking out in daft giggles! Flora sat with her Lucy on her knee beside 'Big Frank' in the van. A placid and easy going creature she never flinched at all the fuss of her loyal owners moving home. She was a princess of cats!

"Is everybody 'Oreight' then?" Frank asked as he prepared to drive us all and Flora's belongings up to Bridge Street.

We all cried out "Yeah!!" as one and Frank put on his tartan flat cap and called out.

"'Reight', then, folks. Sweetly House, here we come!"

Sweetly House was only a few streets away from Steel Road. The home Flora Palmer had lived happily for the past; God knows how many year's!

At Sweetly House Flora made her large one-bedroom flat cosy and as homely as only she could. The place was a residential home. The other residents ranged in age from between 60 and the eldest being 101 year's young. Mrs P had the use of a modern launderette, function and dining room's as well as her own plot of a garden. She was still able to see clearly Steel Road and could often be seen waving to Frank at the good old 'Shakey'!!

Between the frost and bleak February of 1964 and Christmas of 1966, life was fantastic!! Charlotte's Art Shop and Café was doing exceptional business. Mrs Minton (nee Manners) had taken on two loyal staff. Flora Palmer baked cakes, scones and delicious butterfly buns for sale. These were a huge hit with the folk of Steelsbridge. Rachel worked full time for Charlotte also as soon as the business became established.

Charlotte sold her own art work as well as giving other young artists a helping hand up. This was something Tara Bailey had once so kindly done for Charlotte through college and later on. At 'Charlotte's', Rachel, Tara and Flora Palmer, all worked together famously. Charlotte dealt with all the art sales. Knowing Tara was always a great source of help and close friendship. Charlotte was so grateful to her old boss and if anything unexpected cropped up within the business, Tara was there!

By the January of the year of 1966 Rachel Greaves was taken on to Charlotte's books full time. She ran the Café side of things. Flora 'P' meanwhile was happy as much as she ever had been at her old Steel Road home. Helping out for a couple of days a week. Flora's old kitchen at Steel Road had become Charlotte's gallery. A place to paint and perfect her work. Then frame all the beautiful art work. Both Charlotte's and those of the Sheffield artists she and Tara would support.

By my 24th birthday on 6 August 1964 I had established myself again as the regular goalkeeper at Steelsbridge Town F.C. That particular pre-season had also proved so memorable! I was so 'chuffed!' The England squad for a friendly against Spain included the name of 'Gary Minton G.K.'! The squad was asked to assemble at Wembley stadium for the game.

The friendly against the Spanish would kick off the England manager's detailed preparations for the 1966 World Cup Finals. The hosts for the world's greatest football tournament would be England. With no need for us to qualify as we were hosting the thing, Manager Joe Taylor had the advantage of having no distractions in the way of qualification and plenty of time to prepare his players. Mr Taylor chose to play friendly matches to assess who he thought fit, talented and mentally tough enough to be included in the final 22-man squad. These matches would be played between the August of 1964 and spring time of 1966. Just a couple of months shy of our first World Cup match at Wembley Stadium.

Joe Taylor, the England manager had shown great loyalty to Leeds Town's goalkeeper, Simon Clifton, who had been his ever present since the 1962 World Cup. Simon deserved his place as he was the most competent keeper in the country with a good number of caps.

Without my knowledge Mr Taylor had been keeping a close eye on me. My performance's obviously impressing him over quite a long time. I had been enjoying my football since the League Cup Final victory. In fact my form had been exceptional since the 1961/62 season for Steels. I was absolutely made up to win the call up for England!

The most joyful day of my life arrived once we had played those friendlies prior to the tournament in England. I was given my place in the 22-man squad for the 1966 World Cup Tournament to be played between Saturday, 29 June and the final on Saturday, 29 July.

Mr Taylor assembled his squad of players but he wasn't too happy! The first friendly game against Spain proved to have a few problems for him. On the eve of the match there was no sign of the Spaniards! Eventually, the news came through that they were all at London Airport. For some reason all their kit and luggage had gone missing! At 9.00 p.m. on the Friday night, Mr Taylor did manage to get in touch with Carlos Torrenzo, who was the Spanish manager. His opposite number was far from happy either!

"Don't worry, Son. Just forget about the kits. Get yourself and your lad's to your Hotel and we will sort everything out," Joe told Spain's young manager.

The England squad were booked into a modest Hotel close to Wembley Stadium and once the boss had been told that Spain had arrived safely at their Hotel. We had a squad meeting. I only knew a few of the England lad's. I had never been great with new folk and needed time to adjust.

Even over the year's at Steels I had chosen to prepare for a match on my own or with the other goalkeeper lad's in our squad. So whichever match I was playing in my career, doing my own thing suited me most of the time.

As the 1966 World Cup progressed I was pleased that I became good friends with Simon Clifton. We trained together and learnt new goalkeeping skills from each other. He was by far a more experienced player than I was but was still open to learning how to improve. So we helped and supported each other even though we were competing to be England No 1 in the World Cup!

As we all assembled in the dining room of the 'Wembley Court Hotel', Joe Taylor entered the room and looked flustered! But his composure and good humour eventually put us all at our ease.

"Right lad's." Mr Taylor said as he sat back in a comfortable big arm chair.

"I've just spoken to the Spanish gaffer Carlos and the match is on! These European's tend to go off the bloody deep end at times. He had been in a bit of a panic and over emotional. I couldn't hear a bloody damn word he was saying on the old 'blower'. On the phone. But I made him understand eventually the match was on. They have managed to get all their kit and luggage back now as far as I could get to know. So that's that little drama over!

Although only a friendly match against Spain I was feeling fantastic! I didn't sleep at all! The adrenalin and joy that raced through me was intense. Time sped by and before I knew it, the match was here. The match itself turned out to be 90 minutes of comedy! After all the confusion Spain ended up having no kit to play in! So Joe Taylor managed to eventually beg, steal and borrow some. Badly fitting for most of their lad's they turned out in the white shirts, Navy blue shorts and white socks that we were famous for wearing as the national team. The second half reminded me of the many a childhood kick about I'd been involved in on the park behind the 'Foxley Estate'. By the blast of the ref's final whistle no one knew who the hell they were supposed to be passing the ball to? This was the most bizarre of games I had ever played in! But both teams had a real laugh and enjoyed what was an unforgettable occasion!

The remaining three friendly matches before the World Cup were pretty ordinary affairs. Simon played in goal for the Scotland fixture away at Ibrox Stadium in Glasgow and against Northern Ireland at Wembley. I was brought back for the game against Wales, also at Wembley Stadium. There was only the one goal in all three games. A penalty which was scored by Tommy Sharpe for us at Ibrox.

As the 1966 World Cup Finals in England approached, Joe Taylor began to dedicate himself to preparing his team and the tactics in great detail. Putting in a lot of hours and gathering masses of information about the teams, we were to face in the first three group matches.

I only saw Charlotte two or three times once the friendly games had been played. This was fine as Charlotte's business had begun to take off and she was extra busy and I had to put my mind to what was the most important time of my footballing career!

I had already had a good send off some weeks before I left for London for the World Cup. Frank had been great and made a big fuss of me! Both Mick and Sammy had written and phoned me to give me their best and I was fit and ready to literally face the world!

England's first group match in the 1966 World Cup on home soil at Wembley was against Poland. The opening match of the whole tournament, following all the opening ceremony.

Back home in Steelsbridge Frank Taylor had decked out the Shakespeare pub in banners, rosettes and flags of red, white and blue! Both inside and out. He handed out rosettes to all his customer's and cup fever had taken over the Valley and the whole of England. The whole of the country!

Mr Taylor had a strict 'No Alcohol' policy for his squad. I had been feeling as soft as a fiddle for a long time and was full of confidence. But I'd made sure I'd enjoyed my last night on the beers a few weeks earlier with good old Frank and everyone in the 'Shakey' back home!

"Reight, shut your Racket!" Frank Taylor had called out in the 'Shakey' Tap Room that last time I was in before the World Cup.

"Well, it's not every day that one of our own goes off and plays in the World Cup. Can't say I'll miss you, old 'Gaz' though." Frank was being as dry and tongue in cheek with his humour as ever.

"He never bloody buys any beer when he's allowed to 'sup' in here anyhow." Frank added as he winked at me and raised his pint high in the air as a loud and jubilant cheer came from all in the 'Shakey' that night!!

"But serious now, lad's and lasses." Frank said as the room fell into quiet again.

"Gaz has done us all in this town bloody proud! But most of all he has done his 'sen' proud 'int' last few years! So let's have your best three cheers for lad now. Oh, and also just to say I will be up early 'int' morning to go out and get some of that 'brasso' or polish stuff ready to make that 'Julie's

Rimeney' World Cup all gleaming when Gaz brings it back to us in month or so. Oh, and Gary's winners medal too, of course. Cheers lad and all the bloody best of British luck to "thee kid!" Old Frank then moved swiftly around his pub. Pint of lager in hand. Clinking this together with each and every one of his loyal customer's. Finally the 'Big Lad' clinked his pint to mine as I was reeling from a little too much 'Shakey' beer that night. I wasn't expecting the huge bear hug he gave me as I stood alone at the Tap Room Bar.

I was up and away early the next morning after the farewell in the 'Shakey' with Frank and everyone. I was relaxed and determined to enjoy my next few weeks. I had slept soundly on the train journey down to London. The Capital City was all a buzz with the World Cup! Kings Cross was beginning to welcome fans from all over the earth. I was like an over excited kid whose Christmas and Birthday's had all come at once!

England had been fortunate. All our first three group matches were to be played at Wembley. A real advantage. The mood of the country that summer was all about football! Even those who didn't usually enjoy or were fond of the game were beginning to get hooked. Everyone was getting caught up in the festival of football in 1966!

Once the tedium of the opening ceremony and the meet and greets with all the high and mighty of the game were done we could all concentrate on kicking off the tournament.

Because Joe Taylor had been suitably impressed with my form for 'Steels' and in those few friendly games for the country he gave me my first full England cap! I didn't know of this until the morning of the Poland game. I was on such a high! I was rested, confident and relishing the beauty and tremendous atmosphere as the 1966 World Cup held in England for the first time got underway!

We were so poor though! Nervous and much too conscious of the expectation from the crowd, ourselves and the country against a very skilful Polish side. We almost tasted defeat. I was quite pleased with some of the saves I needed to make. In particular in the first half. One in which I had to leap high to claw the ball from out of the air and another in which I prevented a certain goal! I had to dive head long to my right-hand side of my goal and palm the ball around the post. Our defence was fragile against Poland!

When the Poles were awarded a penalty ten minutes from the end of the match the crowd fell silent. After scoring from the spot, the England crowd turned hostile against us, as we headed for defeat! Apart from playing the long ball we were without a clue what to do. So with only a couple of minutes left and the fans leaving the Wembley terraces in droves we managed to rescue a point. This was a very messy goal. So the start of the most important tournament the country had ever seen was lack lustre and disappointing for us all.

The remaining two group games thankfully were to tell a different story. We settled our nerves and overcame Switzerland by two goals to nil and in an inspiring performance against Hungary we delighted the fans with a spectacular 3.0 victory!

Our manager, Joe Taylor, was determined! Protecting his England squad being his most important task. Avoiding any distractions. Distractions such as dealing with the press and the media. We were also advised to have little contact with our loved ones until the end of the 1966 World Cup.

We were all 'chuffed' when told that we were to play our next match at Wembley Stadium! So staying at our Hotel nearby. We had our privacy there and to be fair to the press and the public they respected us in this way.

"Right lad's." Joe said as he chose to make himself comfortable in his bright blue armchair at our Hotel. This chair was to bring out the superstitious side in the boss. Always settling down in her for these vital team talks.

"We are going to forget that 'debacle' against Poland!" Joe told us calmly, knocking dregs of ash and tobacco from his pipe before refilling this with fresh tobacco.

"So we have Chile next lad's." Mr Taylor said as he drew gently on his pipe before glancing up through the bluey, grey smoke swirling above.

"Wednesday night, 4 July. Tomorrow night will be our toughest challenge yet. They will be tricky these South Americans. Make no mistake about it. Gary Minton!" The boss said out loud in his commanding voice. I had been hanging on his every word. The boss had a way of always holding your attention and I listened. But when I heard my name, I began to feel uneasy and in awe of the man.

"Yes, Mr Taylor." I said.

"You don't talk to our defence enough, lad. You are too mute. Now I need more vocals from you. Get your back four organised, lad! Otherwise you're doing a fine job. Well done." Mr Taylor then winked at me and then went through telling the rest of the lad's what he needed from them and gave similar praise too.

"Now get out of my sight!" he said in a jovial way. "I'm off to have me afternoon kip. Oh, and just give everything you have got. Heart and Soul. We are coming along nicely." He added.

We all made ourselves more comfortable at the Wembley Court Hotel. I was really pleased we were staying so close to Wembley Stadium. I was settled there and got myself into a nice routine each and every day. Confidence was bubbling along nicely amongst the squad. We were blessed in not having picked up any injuries. This meant we had a healthy competition for places which also suited the boss.

I was given the nod to start against a very strong Chile side. On a filthy, wet and foggy Wednesday night, the South American's proved to be our toughest test yet. Throughout a gruelling 90 minutes tempers flared up! Both sides determined to progress to the quarter finals of the World Cup of 1966! Our midfield was bossed by Jimmy Gold! But he was giving as good as he got by Chile's Hugo Santana who was a fine Captain, having won dozens of caps for his country over the year's. Both Jimmy and Santana clashed heads half way through the second half! This was a pure accident! After a lengthy stoppage for treatment, respective substitutes were used. There leaving the field was a big blow for both teams. After this, there were few chances created. Not until ten minutes from time when we finally struck gold! Arthur Harvey, England's young left winger, danced through the Chilean defence. The Fulham lad hit a swerving gem of a shot. The ball crashing into the back of the net! Chile were distraught as their players fell in despair to their knees to the Wembley turf! Meaning we had secured a quarter final place!

Following the hard-fought victory over Chile, Joe Taylor was showing signs of feeling pressure! Three of our key players had picked up injuries. Jimmy Gold was feeling the effects of his head clash with the Chilean skipper. Meanwhile our Captain, Bobby Giles, an experienced full back for Manchester Town had limped off having suffered a dead leg. He limped off with only five minutes to the ref's final whistle after the heavy challenge. The boss was also really concerned about our centre forward. Tommy Sharpe of Leeds City had broken his right leg the previous season. Having worked hard to regain full fitness, Tommy earned his place in the World Cup squad. But in the three group games and in particular against Chile, he was reluctant to get into the action in the full-blooded way as before his fracture of the leg. The boss was frustrated that Tommy didn't put himself about in the opposition penalty area and make a real nuisance of himself! In particular, when England created chance's at corner's and set pieces.

The week between the win over Chile and the quarter final, we left nothing to chance. The boss had us doing intensive training!

On the eve of our quarter final with France, again we were lucky in being able to play at Wembley. Joe gave us some rest bite. Some time to relax and not have our minds overtaken by the tournament. But nothing more than going to bed for an early night was the choice for the majority of our squad.

Between the Chile and French ties, Tommy Sharpe was given some thorough workouts. The boss had given Tommy some great advice, telling him he would be making him substitute for the encounter with France. The manager told young Tommy that Roy Goldman was to play centre forward. Goldman at 29 had also once fractured his right leg some nine years before. He had a long battle to get back into full fitness.

For two-and-a-half-year's Roy had been determined and dedicated in winning his place back for both club and country. But throughout this time, Joe Taylor had been a massive support to Roy in making sure he regained the sharpness and suitable attitude to play top class football once again. Thanks to Joe. Roy Goldman had overcome his fear of further injury once he began to play again and Roy's confidence returned. Which was the crucial thing. Once this confidence returned, so the goals came flooding back!

By the time England walked out at Wembley to face France, Jimmy Gold and our Captain, Bobby Giles, were fit once again. The week's grace between rounds had done them both the world of good!

On a warm and oppressive night at Wembley Stadium, France played well. Slick passing and confidence had brought them through the group stages. They had not even conceded a single goal in the tournament so far. All the fine-tuned preparation from Joe Taylor was rewarded. Our defence was strong and determined. I had little to do during the French game. But I still had to keep alert and continued to keep yelling at my back four to keep them on their toes also. Acting upon the 'pep talk' the boss had given me.

"KEEP ON YOUR TOES, LAD'S!" I shouted out. "BOB, KEEP 'EM STRONG!" To our skipper Bobby Giles!

A crowd of over 100,000 were at the quarter final. The noise was tremendous and ear splitting! Not just when there was a chance of either team scoring but all the time! I had never ever experienced anything like this in all my football career. The shivers through my spine and adrenalin rush was amazing! Funnily enough, the first 45 minutes were dull. The crowd's passion being the only talking point.

At half-time in the Wembley dressing room, Mr Taylor sat with his body curled over the back of an old chair, waiting while all our laughter and banter had come to an end. Staring far ahead at the old grand marble clock which dominated one wall of the Wembley Home Team Dressing Room. Then he let us all have an almighty dressing down!!

"I DON'T KNOW?!!!" He shouted out at us all. His voice to shake the whole stadium!

"I DON'T KNOW WHAT THE 'FULK' YOU ARE ALL SO 'FULKING' HAPPY ABOUT!?" "WHAT THE HELL DO YOU THINK YOU ARE ALL PLAYING AT!!!?" Then a 'titter' and 'guffaw' from our Captain, Bobby Giles made the boss go scarlet in the face!! He came from behind the chair and his fury meant us all having to escape the dressing room! Bob really should have known better! But I don't think none of us had seen Joseph Taylor in such a state of rage before! Not even Bobby who had played under the gaffer for many a year. Football boots, tea cups and whatever else the boss could get his hands on went flying through the air! No one was hit by anything but we were frightened half to death! Another long glance at the old marble, Wembley clock did calm down Joe though. Standing there with hands clasped behind his back and straightening his Navy-blue tie with the England crest proudly displayed, Mr Taylor composed himself.

"Right were due back out there in five minutes. So listen up now, you lot! I'm not picking anyone of you out in particular for not giving a shit because that's easy! I'm telling you all right now that we either start playing like we know we can or else we are 'fulking' well going home!! So stop pissing about and give it your all." Mr Taylor then went over to one of the dressing room sinks to wash his face before turning around to say one last thing to us.

"Oh, and by the way, 'SHARPEY' you're on and don't bloody let me down. 'HAYLEY', you're of!."

So with a now 3:3:4 formation and our best two strikers of Ray Goldman and Tommy Sharpe in tandem up front, we again ran out on to the Wembley pitch.

I'm not sure France knew what had hit them in that second half! The half seemed to speed by in just a couple of minutes! I think I touched the ball only a couple of times? I think these were all back passes. A lovely worked goal from Tommy Sharpe gave us the confidence to go on and secure a well-deserved 2:0 victory! Tommy was a brave as an England Lion! Throwing himself between the French full backs! His header screaming high into the roof of the net! Tom then ran on over to Len Fleet, whose perfect right-wing cross had given him the superb headed goal. An exquisite one – two between Sharpe and Roy Goldman then puzzled the French. Golman struck a shot which hit the crossbar. But their stranded goalkeeper could do nothing about Roy Goldman heading the ball home!

The quarter final against France was the best that we played by far throughout the World Cup of 1966!! Tommy Sharpe was the man of the match! His bravery in heading home our first goal and his overall work rate in tackling and covering the Wembley pitch was a magnificent effort by him!

"You did OK. I Suppose." Our boss, Joe Taylor, said very much tongue in cheek as we all got back to the dressing room that night.

"Keep It Up." The gaffer added before he straightened his three lions tie in the mirror then walked out of the room. He was determined to keep us on our toes! But from his body language, as he walked out, I could see that he was the proudest and most delighted man in England!

We had time now to rest and prepare for our next crucial World Cup tie. The teams left in the competition were now sitting up and taking notice of us at last! But we the players, the press, the fans and the whole country were well aware that our next opponents were going to be the most difficult yet. West Germany were the current holders of the famous 'Jules Rimet Trophy'. Four years before in Berlin they had beaten a very useful Chile to lift the golden prize. The match being hailed as the greatest of all the World Cup's played before. The Germans winning 3:2 following extra time. West Germany had managed to keep pretty much the same squad from the 1962 tournament. But they had been hit hard by injury through this World Cup and only just qualified from the group stage. But in the quarter final at Leeds Town's Elland Park, they really turned it on in playing some sensational football as they demolished Uruguay by 5 goals to 0!

The Sunday before the crucial Semi Final, Mr Taylor said we should spend some valuable time with our families. I hadn't seen Charlotte since well before the World Cup began. She came down to London and had a lovely surprise for me!

"We are so proud of you love. You have done ever so well." Charlotte said. We both embraced and kissed and talked for a long time just as if we hadn't seen each other for years. Charlotte had booked into the very same Hotel that we had spent such a great time on our honeymoon some year's before. She booked herself in there for ten days.

"I have a really lovely surprise for you Gaz." Charlotte said with a coy smile as we strolled on the pathway by the Serpentine in Hyde Park. The sun was shining brightly on that hot summer's July day. We were both so happy and calm as we walked hand in hand through the Park.

"Don't tell me you have brought the whole of Steelsbridge along with you?" I said as I gave her a nudge as if to make her fall into the lake.

"Not quite." She replied smiling as she brushed back her silky raven black hair from her eyes. Charlotte then all of a sudden pointed over to a couple who were sat a few yards away. An elderly lady and gent who were feeding the pigeons and waving away to us both.

"Jack! Alice! God! What the! What are you doing here?

Wow! Great to see you both!" I said as I shook them warmly by the hands. I then then found myself hugging them too!

"'Aye', lad. I 'wi' wondering what had happened to 'ye?' Somebody had told us there 'wa' a World Cup on in this 'wee' little town." Old Jack was being as dry and matter of fact as ever. Jack then made space on their park bench for Charlotte and myself to sit down. I then sat next to Alice.

Alice Burroughs was a sweet and quiet lady. Always letting her actions speak out with a quiet reassuring word for anyone who she thought needed help was her way.

"Are you OK, lad?" Alice asked me as Jack and Charlotte chatted away happily next to us. We had all been overcome by all the events of the past few weeks. The football had even got Charlotte hooked! She wasn't usually all that interested in the game. Meanwhile Jack had always looked forward to the summer months to being able to leave all the headache's the season before had brought him! Alice Burroughs was such a kind soul. But there was always the sense of loneliness and longing I thought from her. That I picked up on her not being all that happy sometimes! This was never from anything she said or that I was aware had happened in her life. I just couldn't really explain this feeling I had when we met or spent some time together. I always experienced similar feelings with Mick's Mum, Julie too. This wasn't anything I had ever discussed with anyone! I didn't really understand myself?

"I'm feeling the pressure a little Mrs B!" I told Alice. She smiled kindly at me then looked across the Hyde Park Lake. Her pale blue eyes taking in all that beauty of the London Park.

"You know lad." Alice then said to me in what was almost a whisper. "I was a dancer a long, long time ago. Long before I'd met Jack even. I was living just around the corner here in London. I was due to give a big performance at the Royal Albert Hall one particular summer. I had been worried sick! I'd almost let all the nerves and the big occasion back then beat me! But that Saturday night turned out to be the most thrilling experience of my life! The best of my life, Son. I was only 18 year's old. Alice then looked to the right side of her in the direction of Knightsbridge. I think all her memories and all those fantastic feelings came flooding back to at that very moment. She then giggled a little just like that 18-year-old girl that was still so vivid to her!

"Enjoy yourself, kid. That is my advice to you now. Life is a short one. Just go out there on that pitch and enjoy every single minute! You will be fine then I promise you will lad." Alice told me so calmly with some moisture beginning to form in her pale blue eyes.

Once we had said goodbye to Jack and Alice in Hyde Park I thought a lot about what Alice Burroughs had said to me. Charlotte was well used to my coming over all silent sometimes by now. She also always knew when I needed to confide in her. Or if I had something important I needed to let her know.

"Are you OK, love?" Charlotte asked me as we walked back through the gates of Hyde Park and along Lancaster Gate.

"Oh, I'm OK, Charlotte. Just been having a word with Alice is all." I said calmly to her.

"Oh yeah. You going to elope with an older woman, Mr Minton?" Charlotte replied, giggling as we held hands to cross the park back to her Hotel.

For the following few days and up until the massive match with the West Germans, I was fine. I just couldn't remember the last time I had been so relaxed and comfortable in my own skin. The little chat I'd had with Alice. Mrs Burroughs and later Charlotte had done me the world of good and had really boosted my confidence!

"Yeah, I know." Charlotte had said later on. "I thought I'd ask her to give you a few words of wise encouragement." That Sunday afternoon had been so special for me.

On 25 July 1966 a capacity Wembley crowd and huge television audience watched as England came up against the formidable West Germany. The sunshine had blessed the Capital City of London all that week. So under the blazing glare of the Wembley Stadium floodlights, everything was all set fair for our Semi final with Germany.

Joe Taylor had said very little this time before we kicked off and we were blessed with being injury free. Fielding the same team as the Semi Final win over France. Conditions were perfect. Not too warm and the Wembley pitch was lush and green and cut short. We had no excuses, neither team had!

We could both turn on the fine play and magic and play our hearts out!

I was very busy against West Germany that night of the Semi Final. I saw a lot of the action! I needed to make a string of difficult saves to keep out the forward line of a very impressive German team! But I was not the only one kept alert! My opposite number Gunter Mahyer had been peppered with shots! He also made a fantastic save! One that I thought was the best I have ever had the pleasure of seeing! Tommy Sharpe had collected the ball just shy of the penalty area. He then ghosted past two German defender's and hit the sweetest low shot which everyone in the stadium and back home watching TV were convinced was going to make the inside of Mahyer's netting bulge! Mahyer at full stretch managed to tip the ball around his far post. As soon as the huge crowd and all the player's had realised he had made the save of the tournament rapturous cheers and applause came from the 100,000 + crowd! This save was also memorable in that this was almost the last action of the Semi Final's 90 minutes.

We were so weary at full time! The match had been played at a ferocious pace! Both teams having produced a real World Cup Semi Final Classic! Joe Taylor knew full well we deserved a short rest.

"Stay on your feet though, lad's. I don't care what that lot are doing over there. Don't whatever you do sit down as well." The boss told us in his commanding voice as he also pointed to the whole West German team all shattered and lying on the Wembley turf as if they were wounded soldiers. All being attended to by their manager and trainer.

"Just keep on moving those limbs, lad's. Keep your bodies supple and most of all think positive. Carry on playing as well as you have done in those 90 minutes and we will definitely be back here for the 'BIG UN' this Sunday. Mr Joe Taylor's words left us upbeat and full of confidence. Leaving a strong impression on us all to see the job through and win a place in the World Cup Final!

With very few chances created in extra time and both teams feeling the strain and in some player's cramp, I received the ball and with a long hard 'punt' up field, I was amazed to see the result! The ball reached the edge of the German goalmouth. The only player that was alert to my huge kick was our left winger, Arthur Harvey. The Arsenal lad then controlled the ball smart as you like before looking up to notice Gunter Mayher had crept well of his goal line. A majestic chip Arthur floated for what seemed a life time over the head of the stranded Mayher before calmly resting in the back of his net! Thunderous cheering and applause along with a mass pitch invasion as the referee blew his Final whistle meant we were through to World Cup Final of the year 1966! The first time this country had reached the Holy Grail of football!

The adrenalin was pumping through me for hours after the Final whistle of our Semi Final. I was living in dream land!

A surreal and weird yet wonderful place! When I was a kid growing up! I dreamt about times such as last night so many times. As I sat in the Wembley dressing room following the Semi Final my vivid green keepers top was wet through with the sweat of those gruelling 120 minutes we had all been through! The calmest person out of all of us was stood looking into the full-length dressing room mirror sipping from a white china cup of hot tea. The proudest and calmest man of them all. Mr Joseph Taylor Esquire!

I slept for 12 long, blissful and peaceful hours that Wednesday night. I woke finding myself giggling just like a child, wondering if the past few weeks had been some kind of dream itself! But as my head cleared and I had a rush of thoughts, I prayed this dream would continue forever!

Brazil had been worthy winners of the Jules Rimet Trophy in the past. But they were lacking confidence and had limped through the group stages of the World Cup in England in 1966'. But with impressive victories in the last 16 against Sweden and again in the quarter and Semi Finals too. To have a chance to claim their third World Cup against us at Wembley.

Sunday 29 July 1966 was an overcast day in London. The rains before the final had given way to bright sunshine. By 2:45 that afternoon I was kicking my football free of mud and the Wembley grass on the foot of my goalpost. Turning around I was enchanted by the sight of the beautiful arching rainbow! An inspiring sight. The German referee, Max Laufer threw the special high into the air. England Captain, Bobby Giles, and Brazilian goalkeeper, Oscar Feelinhio, shook hands and gave each other a friendly hug. The Wembley pitch was so greasy! The rain had given us the ideal conditions to pass and fizz the football around in a fine way. This of course suited the Brazilians too.

Over 120,000 supporters roared and sang their hearts out as we kicked off. The streets of England were deserted due to this World Cup Final spectacle.

Both teams were affected by nerves. I received far too many back passes than I was comfortable with. An example of the fear that had won us over in the first 20 minutes or so of the final. The only goal bound chance of the first half fell to Brazil when Revilinio pounced on a slack back pass from one of our defenders. The usually commanding Johnny Wright guilty of a rare lapse in concentration. I managed to make a save by diving at full stretch to palm the ball around my near post!

"Relax, lad's for 'FULKS 'sake!" was Mr Taylor's response as we came into the dressing rooms at half time. Then adding, "Spray the football around this big pitch. Use all that Wembley has to offer you, lad's. Come On, Now. Oh, and you back four, lot. 'STOP PASSING THE BLEEDING BALL BACK TO GAZ IN THE NET ALL THE TIME! I don't want Gary to have anything to do second half. Well, Done Lad's Though!" Joe then gave each and every one of us a huge pat on the back before he put on his overcoat and led us out again for the second half of the final. He then put on his black pork pie hat and jogged off to the dug outs in front of the Royal Box.

I had next to nothing to occupy me for the rest of the final! But still this can be the hardest part of being a goalkeeper at whatever level. I still had to put family, friends, the crowd and the huge occasion out of my mind and still concentrate in case Brazil came back at me on the counter attack. I studied with the intensity every move we made!

All from the semi-circle on the edge of my goalmouth!

Brazil began to be lethargic but still showed their usual elegance and flair on the ball, which was always their trademark way of playing.

As the rain began to pound down on to the Wembley turf a long high kick out of my hands with just ten minutes of the final remaining again reached to the edge of the Brazilian penalty area. Their Captain Feelinio looked to be a safe pair of hands. I and everyone else in the ground thought him comfortable in being able to pluck the bright orange casey ball out of the air! But then out of nowhere at all Brazilian centre back Paulistau headed the ball right out of his skipper's grasp! The sodden ball then took an age to float up high before settling in the back of Brazil's goal!! Tommy Sharpe and the rest of us lads were all on our way back to our positions waiting for Feelinio to simply boot the ball back up the field deep into our half. I had long since turned my back on play as I then heard the almighty roar and jubilant loud cheering of the capacity Wembley crowd!! This sent me into a real state of panic and confusion! For a couple of unreal moments, none of this was real. Then in astonishment I realised we had just broken the deadlock!!

With just ten minutes of the 1966 final left both teams were stunned! Our celebrations were sedate. Tommy Sharpe shuffled over to weakly shake Roy Goldman by the hand with a non-plused glare on both their faces! I had been counting down all the minutes to the referee's final whistle. When I finally realised what had happened I was seen to be doing a jig and dance all around my penalty box! Then there was further pandemonium from everyone! The crowd, the England bench and, of course, the whole country would have been in raptures then as we all suddenly realised what had been achieved!

Heated arguments broke out between the Brazilian players soon after our goal! Their goalkeeper, Captain Edson

Paulistau, almost coming to blows with his defence. These disruptive moments just after our crucial winner meant the poor German ref was completely puzzled. Max Laufer was that confused he ended totally losing track of time as he was to play a further 10 minutes of the 90 of this amazing 1966 World Cup Final. Not until this World Cup Tournament's statistics had been recorded a long time later did anyone realise that Mr Laufer had played these long extra minutes.

When finally the match was all over, the Boss Joe Taylor came sprinting on to the Wembley Stadium pitch! Throwing off his black pork pie hat high and handsome into the London sky!! The way Joseph Taylor dashed around Wembley that memorable day was an amazing site for all to see! He was just like an excited young kid, whose birthday, Christmas and this wonderful 1966 World Cup win had all come along at once! His huge grin from cheek to cheek lighting up that miserable London rainy Sunday! The big black, heavy overcoat was off his back and his arms were waving high above his head!

The youngest of our World Cup winning team was Frank Haley, who was sat on the centre circle, drained and with his muddy socks and boots off! He had his mouth wide open, white as a sheet and looking like he had seen ghostly footballers all over the Wembley Stadium. Shaking his head one minute and in hysterics the next!

I just could not wait to experience the most fantastic moments of my young life!

"Terribly well done young man!" She said to me in the poshest voice that I had never ever heard anyone, a man, a woman or child say to me ever before! Oh! The shock! Oh my God! I was literally bloody speechless meeting her! I knew how overcome with beautiful emotion young 'Hals'! had just been now. I was just staring gob smacked at this woman who I had only ever seen on television before. She was like something so unreal! Immaculate in her woollen, Navy blue trouser suit. Her hat, dainty and of a creamy colour! But what will always stay with me until the end of my days though about Her Majesty Queen Elizabeth the Second was she had such pale kind eyes. Her poise and humility also shone through to me. But she is Royal after all.

"Oh, I'm so sorry, Mrs…Mrs…Queen…Ms…Mrs…eh…ah…" I said or didn't say as was the case. She removed her long, perfect white gloves and I could feel the red blush of embarrassment in my face! I just couldn't stop apologising. I then just wanted to receive my magnificent winner's medal! Eventually with this golden prize firmly in my hands. I stumbled down the 39 steps from the Royal Box!

"You, soft young sod! Fancy leaving 'thee' bloody goaly gloves on… You are priceless, lad!" I then became confused that Bobby Giles had said this to me in such a joyful way. He then continued to chuckle away and kiss his own winner's medal over and over again!

"Anyway, Bob, what the Fulk are you all doing standing down here? You should be up there, Captain, picking up World Cup from Mrs Windsor up there!" I shouted out loud! As I looked back at Bobby and the rest of our team. They were all applauding so hard and looking up to the Royal Box! Our Skipper Bobby Giles gulped and choked back on the emotion he was clearly feeling! Clutching his small maroon box, containing his hard-won medal!

As we all looked up to the splendour of the Royal Box, Her Majesty, the Queen of England, was keeping hold of Joe Taylor's hand for such a long time! But she eventually handed him the 'GOLDEN PRIZE' we had all been so preoccupied with for so long!! They both seemed to be chatting away to one another as if they had known each other all their lives as the players, crowd and every other soul at Wembley Stadium that July Sunday of 1966 just weren't there at all! But the World was and it was so wonderful too!

Chapter 11

That night following the 1966 final celebrations burst out all over London and the rest of the country! We were to finally reach our Wembley Court Hotel at God knows what time? Once we had all got changed and boarded the coach, we parked up. The crowds along Wembley Way were breath taking! There was a sea of red white and blue flags, banners and rosettes and the noise was tremendous! Rattles were being twirled over the supporter's heads! They were all singing their hearts out with choruses of ENGLAND! ENGLAND! ENGLAND! Then the fans there would belt out the National Anthem with Gusto!

I vaguely remember Mick, Sammy, Charlotte and Rachel meeting up with me. We later fell and danced our way through the jubilant London streets! We sat on the Majestic Lions at the base of Nelsons Column. Then jigged our way along Piccadilly Circus. All of us saluting the love Statue of Eros over and over again! I remember diving head long into the Trafalgar Square fountains with Mick and Sammy and God knows how many other proud and ecstatic England fans!!!

The next thing I recall we were back at Wembley Hotel as three of us woke up in our unmade bed together! Charlotte, myself and the grand and Golden 'Jules Rimet Trophy' nestling in the middle of us!

That week before Christmas of 1966 was a sad time. We were all brought crashing down to earth with a real sense of shock!

"Oh! no! no! no! Oh dear God no!" Charlotte was ashen faced! holding on tightly to the back of Flora's old rocking chair!

Charlotte had found Flora Palmer in her art gallery! In the old kitchen where our dear old friend had spent a large part of her life. 'Lucky', her devoted black cat was dozing and purring in her lap.

"She looks so peaceful, Gary love! Oh! I'm not sure I can deal with…take all this in!" Charlotte said choking back her tears.

Flora Elizabeth Palmer's funeral service was a huge event! The most moving of occasions. One which the small town of Steelsbridge had never seen the likes of before!

On 23 December 1966, St Pauls Church in Smithsly Village was struggling to hold all those mourners who wanted to pay their respects as Flora's coffin was brought out and placed in the hearse. Friends she had known whilst working in London in her 20s, along with all the locals of the Valley she had known and forged a long and loving affection came to celebrate a remarkable ladies life! Hymns as well as joyful, lively music gave Flora's service a balance of appropriate choices.

I was asked to say a few words which was something I had little to no experience of before. Charlotte and Frank Taylor had also offered to pay tribute to their lifelong friend. I simply thanked everyone for coming along and added how Flora had always been there for us all in the Valley through all the many ups and downs of this life. Charlotte and Frank had made public speeches in the past. Sometimes Charlotte did so at work presenting her paintings to a potential customer. She was to give a lovely and touching tribute.

"There was no pretending with Flora." Charlotte began to say. "If she heard you were struggling, she would be the first to offer her help. She would also search for anything anybody needed from her shop. But what was best of all Flora would tell you straight if you were to ask her advice. If she thought I needed some 'cruel to be kind' words, then that was what she gave you? I had found a friend for life in lovely Flora! God bless you, my love."

Charlotte's so kind words were met with a ripple of applause as she herself sat back down next to me. Just as she did so, she wiped away a small tear with her handkerchief she had taken from my suit's jacket top pocket.

Frank's words were also so charming and kind. The big man had dressed up in his finest clothes! A Navy blue and lemon waistcoat and tie did his dear old friend proud.

"Well, then I can't 'reight' believe it of the old 'lass' to leave me with one less customer now." Frank began as a few giggles and soft respectful laughter broke out amongst everyone!

"Anyhow, I've known Mrs P all my days there's not a better mate or finer 'lass' 'tha' could ever wish to meet in this whole 'barmy' world of ours. She would give you her last penny and she'd tell you straight if you ever managed to upset her at all. Just as Charlotte said there." Frank then took a sip of water from his glass before carrying on.

"I remember once when I first took on the pub and she walked on in. I think it must have been one of the first times I'd spoke to her. I'm not sure for now." 'Na', then big lad she'd said to me after she'd taken a seat on one of the high chairs at the bar. I know you will make a go of this place. It's never been up to much mind! But it's probably only decent pub 'int' Valley. But be warned 'Big Un'. If you don't give this your best shot, I'll be in here 'wi' more words of wisdom until you get the place ship shape. Now then what you having? I'm buying? Then she just winks at me. 'Aye', I've spent some grand afternoons taking all about her times in London. Me, when I was a 'Nipper'. Oh, all sorts of stuff. So thanks to you all for a 'reight' good turn out for our Flora here today. I know you all thought world of her – just as I did. "CHEERS MRS P!" Frank said as he raised glass of water and came to sit back down at the front.

Flora Palmer's wake in the Shakespeare Tavern was a big celebration! Her beautiful black cat 'Lucky' was treated like a princess of cat's. As she was fed the best fish and pampered by all in the pub. Lucky and Charlotte found solace with each other and now we are both the proud owners of her.

I spent a quiet Christmas with Charlotte that year of 1966. We had long since given the 'Shakey' Christmas Eve's a miss. We did call in though for an hour to see good old Frank around tea time. Then we dropped in on Evie and Julie before returning home. We then had a nice, quiet night in. Going off to our bed as I had training for 'Steels' the next day, which I had been used to for many years now, having always played on Boxing Day.

On New Year's Eve of 1966, I suddenly began to feel dreadful as soon as I woke!

"Christ, Gary, you look like death warmed up, love." Charlotte had told me that morning. Once I'd looked in the bedroom mirror, I had to agree. I even scared myself with sweat pouring out of me. My blonde shorn hair was wet through. My pale blue eyes lifeless. I lacked colour at the best of times but there was an ashen hue to me. I ended up falling back into our bed, sleeping for the next 12 hours and eventually waking in 1967!

"Christ, Charlotte love, you like death…warm…"

Charlotte pushed me aside in a playful way before saying,

"Oh, OK, clever Sod, so I've gone and got your 'Lurgy' now."

"Thank you very much, aha…ah…"

By the time we had both began to feel something like human beings again, we learnt that 'Steelsbridge' had been sick too. The nasty virus going around that New Year had affected most folk unfortunately.

"Bloody plague! I thought that 'wa' it for yours truly." Frank had said all jokey and grim faced when we had called in to see if he was OK a week or so into January of 1967.

"I know, Frank. I had to miss a couple of 'Steels' matches and, Charlotte, shut up the shop for ten days." I replied.

"I really did think I 'wa gonna peg out', Gaz lad. I swear to God 'wa' in a 'reight tacking'." Frank said to me with a strange mix of the serious and mischief about him. He always tended to be a bit of a drama King, our Frank, at times.

That nasty virus triggered off what was to be a rough couple of years for us. I kept picking up injuries all the time. Lost my form and became dejected and disheartened with football altogether.

By the end of the 1969/70 season, 'Steels' had escaped relegation by only a solitary point.

Charlotte's business was beginning to haemorrhage money left, right and centre, which by early 1970 meant she had made a loss for the first time since starting up her shop, gallery and café business. The gallery takings were the hardest hit due to poor Flora's passing. Flora had been a real hit with Charlotte's customer's as the money that came in from her baking and general guidance from her business and life experience had left a negative effect but by the December of 1968 another blow came to Charlotte – one she had never seen coming!

Rachel Greaves and Charlotte Minton (nee Manners) had been through difficult childhood's because they had both been brought up in the same children's home – the 'Rose House' – a huge Victorian pile ran by nuns – a place situated on the Man Moor Estate. Which was a deprived area of Sheffield. A poor suburb of the City where a reporters shilling would more than tempt folks living there to brighten their mundane lives.

Rachel had always been the more outgoing of the two close friends. Charlotte more reserved and sensitive as a child anyway. Rachel had the long, golden, flowing locks, very pale blue eyes and a slim figure. She had always been protective of Charlotte!

The autumn of 1968 was a challenging time for Charlotte

"Charlotte, can I chat with you when we are less busy, please, love?" What eventually came out of Rachel asking Charlotte this question was to put a great strain on both Charlotte and our relationship together?

Once Charlotte had finished at her work one day she came home and was worn out. Her long black raven hair and usually immaculate look was suffering a little – her complexion too.

"Charlotte, what is it love?" I asked of her as we sat down in the living room to relax that evening.

"Rachel has dropped a right bloody bombshell on me today, Gary. She has only gone and accepted another job offer at an orphanage she used to work at once. I have always known she was supportive of the kid's homes. But…! Oh, Fulk It!"

Charlotte had finally hit a wall as far as her business was concerned. Rachel's news the last straw in a way to her.

By 1970 I had been really struggling at 'Steels' and by the end of the 1966/67 football season, my form was suddenly beginning to desert me!

Jack Burroughs had also been finding himself under pressure after he had long since promised Steels would have success but as almost 9 year's manager had only brought the 1964 League Cup triumph Jack was told at the start of 1967 that this was by no means good enough.

The Chairman and the board began a big shake up. They gave Jack Burroughs's permission to dive into the transfer market. Generously helping Jack bring the kind of team to Steelsbridge Town, which could be able to lift the First Division Championship!

By the August of 1967 my place in the 'Steels' team was fragile! Jack had kept the faith with me but by Christmas time I had only played the five times with injury and some basic goalkeeping errors along with some sheer bad luck I was to move on from the club I had served since being a youngster of 16. With this major shake up at the club I was asked to see the gaffer again!

"'Ye' having a 'wee' rough patch, laddy?" Jack asked very solemn that day. He seemed very preoccupied to me.

"Oh, you know, boss, I can't seem to keep goal like I used to." I said.

"'Aye'." Jack replied.

"OK, lad. I am going to loan out a few of the lad's. 'Yeself' and Jimmy Cole along with Tom Fry. I 'wa' thinking you could all do 'wi' a 'wee' change. If 'ye' know what I mean, lad?"

I travelled up the M1 to Leeds with Jimmy Cole. Jimmy had come to his last season. He'd had a long career – to be an exceptional servant for 'Steels' over many year's but the old body had betrayed him now. But Jack was giving him one last 'hurrah' at Leeds Town!

I had suffered two serious injuries in my football career. The first one put me back a full season and half. Back during the 1959/60 season we had travelled in midweek up to Carlisle. That December night was drenched in fog. In the second half I sprinted from my goal line. The Carlisle forward had latched on to a long hopeful ball. He was then able to come towards my goal. I then came out and slid feet first at the football, which I not only missed altogether but left their striker flying through the freezing night air! I suddenly then began to feel sick and dizzy! My left leg was placed in a splint! This was the last I remember before passing out!

After 7 days in Carlisle General Hospital, where I underwent an operation. I came on home. I had shattered my left leg. I was in plaster at home for two months! I then had further treatment in the Sheffield Infirmary. This was to repair a fracture of my tibia and fibia!

The irony was that the second time I suffered a fracture I was playing at Linden Park. I was still adjusting to my loan spell with Leeds Town.

The supporters at 'Steels' gave me a lovely welcome! Leeds were stuck at the foot of Division One by the time this fixture came along against 'Steelsbridge Town'.

Leeds Town were to collect their first two points of the season on that mild day in the early December of 1967. I had so little to do in the match which was a really drab 0:0 draw.

On the way out of Linden Park that evening I just didn't notice some grease outside of the dressing room. In fact I wasn't sure what exactly made me fall really? But when I did so I put my right hand to the floor to try to break my fall! So I was to make another journey to the Hospital and endured another lengthy spell out of football through injury.

By 1970 Charlotte was in trouble! The business had become smaller. She chose to close the café side. The Art Gallery and her producing original work became her only income. But by 1974 the inevitable needed to be faced!

Charlotte's business of the past six years was no more!

We converted the house. What had been the business became just a home for us. The downstairs reverting back to our living room, dining room and kitchen. My wages from the football then became our only source of income!

The previous year of 1969 was full of nostalgia and fun for both myself and Charlotte! Mick had left the Navy in 1966. The work he had managed to find in 'Civvy Street' just didn't suit him at all. A Sports Centre in Portsmouth did take him on but he yearned for home. Since leaving the forces Mick had been listless! He had gained weight and then found the bars and clubs of 'Pompey' far too much of a temptation!

From the early summer of 1968 until the New Year of 1969, Mick decided to get his head down and work at his fitness. He would return to being the lad he once was! The fitness he had been blessed with throughout his naval training had returned!

I ended up having a word with Jack Burroughs's and then with help from some of the lad's. Mick was back at 'Steels'!

He began by playing in midfield for the reserves. He then worked hard and eventually broke into the first team!

Mick Joyce played most of the 1969/70 season for Steelsbridge Town. At 29 year's old he was a tremendous asset to the team. His flair and command in the centre of the field led to a real positive. He was chuffed to bits to be then made Captain.

Our social life in the Valley also improved. Mick and his Mum, Julie, along with Aimee, Evie and Sally joined us in having some really memorable times! Then another welcome surprise came along. Sammy returned. Spending the summer months back in the Valley with his folks at their Smithsly Village Cottage.

From the May of 1970 until the start of the 1970/71 football season, history was to pretty much to repeat itself! All through Mick's generosity and ideas to be able to help out the Sheffield Children's Hospital!

My loan spell with Leeds Town came to an end. Or rather my heavily bandaged hand meant that I needed to return home. Although my hand wasn't as serious as when I had broken my leg. The healing process took a very long time! I didn't turn out in goal again until that season of 1969/70. Money was so tight after the Christmas of 1969 that Charlotte was out of work and I just about managed to make what savings we did have seen us through until the August of 1970. The fact that Mick had returned to Valley life was a real blessing. Helping us both out when the bills were getting so much out of hand!

One May night of 1970 Charlotte asked if I'd like to go on over to the pub for a while?

"It's been such a long time since we have been out, love. Shall we just pop on over to see how Frank's getting on?"

"Even though Wednesday nights had always been quiet, we found that the opposite was the case and that we were to have one the best nights in year's at the 'Shakey!'

"What will you have World Cup Hero?" Frank asked. "They're on me lad." he then added.

Ever since the heady days at Wembley in 1966 Frank Taylor had refused to take any money from us! Charlotte always protested and would leave a note on his bar! But I would always find this money being forced back on to me. Good old Frank also had a photo behind his bar. He had bought a replica World Cup and I had posed for a photograph with him with this replica. Daft Frank was holding the Cup on my head with a big, proud, cheesy grin! He had also asked me and the rest of the England lad's to sign this photo for him. Framed and polished everyday this was Big Frank's pride and joy! This had pride of place in the centre of the wall behind Frank's Tap Room Bar.

As the night slowly developed we were to meet with all friend's past and present from a near empty pub at 7.00 p.m. until the early hours of Thursday. The night was a real joy. By 10.00 p.m. Mick had organised something special in by what was then a packed Shakespeare Tavern. Laughter, tears and many stories were told. Mick and Sammy Chivers arrived full of the joys of spring! Soon followed by Julie Joyce and

Aimee. Then Sally and Evie who neither I nor Charlotte had seen for such a long time!

By 1970 Frank had changed the Shakespeare Tavern. Where there had once been seating along the walls of the Tap Room he had chosen to put in a separate seating area with booths, tables and glass partitions around each.

That particular Wednesday night I sat with Sammy and Mick. Meanwhile Charlotte and Julie along with Aimee and Evie sat together at the opposite side of the Tap Room.

"So, Sammy lad and Gaz, what's new, lad's? Fancy meeting you two in here again!" Mick winked at us both as he said this before supping his pint of lager in one swift go!

"Now Gaz, now Mick, lad. Don't forget 'World Cup Winner!" Sam said chuckling and pointing his forc finger above my head.

"Oh yeah!" Mick suddenly cried out with glee as he almost dropped his empty beer glass to the floor! "Forgot all about that, mate." He then added and began to chuckle more. We all then burst out laughing which just reminded me of so many times I had been in the 'Shakey' with the lad's over the year's! Especially when we had all been teenagers.

"Free jukebox, lad's and lasses. Don't say I never 'gi' me punters 'out'!" Frank told us as he took the empty pots from all our tables, stacking them high and adding more until he reached his bar once again.

"'Tha' never gi…" Mick tried to blurt out.

"Don't bloody bother Joyce. You know I'm the most generous Landlord in this shabby old town!" Frank piped up as an interruption and comical jest. Again laughter filled the room. Just after this the crash of glasses meant Frank had lost control of his stack of pint pots again! He was then heard to call out.

"Dust Pan and brush, love. I've gone and done me usual trick!" One of the bar staff then came along to help Big Frank out.

Taking advantage of the free juke box, Aimee chose to select some tunes. The other girls made space in the centre of the room so they could all dance along. Which they did until falling into their booth giggling!

Aimee had been through a lot ever since she had first been poorly that night of our wedding. Operations and long stays in the Children's Hospital were a regular interruption to her young life. But now we were all so delighted as she looked so well. Now fourteen year's old she was slim and beautiful. She had been given another chance at life and was going to enjoy this to the full having been discharged from Doctor Brameld's care.

Aimee and Craig Brameld had become good friends since 1961. Both continuing to raise funds for the children in Sheffield, where Aimee spent most of her time now. Their help for kids all over the U.K and in particular those who were admitted to the Children's had been crucial! Aimee had even spoke to her Mum and Mick about a career in nursing.

During our get together in the 'Shakey' that night Mick and Frank had requested quiet. Mick then picked up the microphone.

"You may think tonight's been just another night in here folks. Well, no. I didn't just hope you would all turn up. I made sure by some crafty planning aha! I have been organising with Mr Jack Burroughs at the football club to try and raise funds for the Children's Hospital where our Aimee does such fantastic work along with all the staff there. We are going to organise a couple of charity football matches this summer at Linden Park. Frank here as plans for a disco every month up until Christmas with raffles and some daft games and that. That's right 'int' it Big Man?"

Mick asked as he turned to Frank.

"Eh…what? Oh…'aye!' What's happening again, Mick lad? Sorry, Son." Frank was miles away, caught up no doubt in the emotions of the night.

"Pay attention, Frank lad, please, will 'ye'?" Mick said patting him kindly on the back.

"Yeah, so I'm open to any other ideas or suggestions, folks. The Sheffield Children's Hospital has done wonders for Aimee and is a marvellous place for all kids who get so poorly. It's a bloody tremendous place and I just can't praise them all enough. 'Best in the world'!"

Mick looked exhausted as he came to the end of what he had to say to us all. Crow's feet under his eyes had been there over the past couple of years. He wiped away a small tear before hugging and then kissing his mother, Julie, and then Aimee before then taking a seat. He chose to sit down alone as he finished his pint and drew heavily on his cigarette! The applause in the Tap Room that night was out of this World. The cheering then seemed to last hours.

Chapter 12

Sammy went back to London just shy of Christmas 1970.

Like a magnet to him. The Capital City attracted his curiosity and bright nature.

Mick had made a decision too by the time Frank had begun decking out the pub with Christmas decorations.

"I've decided to come back to the Valley for good." He said.

But I was really pissed off with Mick at this time. Overhearing him telling one of the lad's in the 'Shakey'. I was puzzled. I thought we had become mates and close again ever since he had come back from down South.

"Oh, don't be so soft, Gary," Charlotte had said to me. "He would have told you. Of course he would have." She added as we were sat at home discussing what I'd overheard in the pub. Hearing this from Charlotte just added further insult. I was biting my tongue, so as not to blurt out the fact that if Rachel had done something similar as they were such close friends. I doubt I would have never have heard the last of such a snub.

By the end of 1970 we were both struggling. Money for Charlotte had become tight. Also I was missing a lot of 'Steels' matches. The cold and harsh winters and my injuries over the years were taking their toll! Charlotte had begun to work at the 'Shakey' pub. Rachel also helped her out with some extra hours at the Children's Home where she had been set on and she still managed to make a little from her paintings and art work.

Mick Joyce organised the Charity Day. Eventually he and the community helped raise thousands of pounds for the children in Sheffield! Everyone worked so hard on and before the Fun Day as well as throughout the year! Mick occupied himself at Linden Park Stadium and helped out. Otherwise by doing odd jobs in the town. He seemed happy and content with his life back home. He had settled back living with his Mum, Julia. I became envious but I also knew more than anyone else that Mick deserved to be happy now! His life had been one of severe ups and downs at times!

The very first 'Fun Day' at Linden Park was magnificent! Mick having really thrown himself into organising of this event after he had been the main ideas man following the announcement in the 'Shakey' that night. Suddenly, Mick was looking fit and well and half his age. He had longer hair. The shock of shorn ginger was no more! An influence to the 1970s time. Having looked so exhausted and spent only the year before. His look of determination and happy lucky attitude suited him.

The Linden Park Stadium by the March of 1971 was looking incredible! The first team and reserves had done a fine job. The main stand had been painted in the 'Steels' colours of sunshine yellow and Navy blue. All the turnstiles, dressing rooms and stands had been given a real face lift!

The fun fair, tombola stall and coconut shy's were set up all over the 'Steels' pitch. Races and all other games took place at the ground too. The pitch was immaculate!

Charlotte, Rachel, Aimee, Evie and Julie Joyce, all had been busy. Cakes, pies, pasties, buns and sweets were all for sale. 'Flora Palmer' helped too! She was there in spirit, of course, she was! The discovery of many of her recipe's written in her beautiful handwriting was a lovely find. All the girls efforts for the Fun Day had been read from Flora's precious cook or recipe books.

Every single penny raised was given over to Aimee and Doctor Brameld by the end of that joyful day of May 12 1971. By 7.30 p.m. that evening the pitch had been cleared for the day's Charity Football Match to start!

"How did you manage that?" I asked Mick as we lined up to applaud.

"I'll tell 'thee' later." Mick said as he was shaking hands with all of the 1966 World Cup Winners. I lead out the 1966 team between two lines of Stocksbridge teams. A kind of guard of honour. Plus the 'Steels' select 11 made up of players. Who had served the club since 1946. The year our football club was formed. Lining up across the way were the current Steels, lad's! So I was to alternate between the two. Shaking hands with them. This caused great hilarity and at one point, thunderous applause from the packed stands all around. Stands packed with loyal 'Steels' fans. Other local's and Hospital staff amongst them.

"Right, lad's. 'Nay', serious play from 'ye' 'toneet'. I want 'ye' all to entertain and raise some big cash for them poorly 'wee' kids!" Having said this to both teams, Jack Burroughs's searched for his ref's whistle. That day he chose to wear an all Navy Scotland kit and looked the perfect official! Jack had kept himself fit over the year's! A stocky, grey-haired gent now. But still more than able to dash around and keep up with men half his age!

Jack blew his whistle and shouted across to his two other officials.

"Come On, 'Jock'! just bloody well get on 'wi' it man, will you?" Frank Taylor hollered out as he stood waving his red linesman's flag.

"Yeah, come on. I'm sodding freezing me 'cods' off over here!" Mick then suddenly called out from the other side.

Running his touchline, Mick thought they were joking at first when they had asked him to do this and carry the yellow linesman's flag. His contribution though was to chat and lark about with the spectators in the stands.

By the end of the Charity Match no one had a clue what the score was? So someone decided to ask Mr Jack Burroughs's, our Scottish referee.

"Aye, well, I lost count 'didny', lad's?" Let's call it a draw. So that's England 42 − Steels 42. It 'dissnay' matter. "We all add a grand time and the kids will all benefit." He said with humour. Then Jack did something I had never seen him do at the end of the match. He went across to Mick and gave him a huge bear hug! Almost crushing the lad's ribs! He then took out a 'wad' of Scottish 'Dosh' from his wallet before he then stuffed this gently into Mick's top pocket of his black linesman's shirt!

"That's for 'ye' Hospital lad." Jack said. "I want to help 'ye' make them poorly kids all better! I just was never ceased to be surprised by old Jack Burroughs's. He could be as hard as nails all the time I'd known him over the year's. But every now and again he would melt your heart. Showing such kindness and gentle thought for others! Then I was so moved as Jack's face became so gentle as a small salty tear was shed."

The Charity Day was still young as back at the Shakespeare Tavern more funds were raised. A great night which by 2.00 a.m. the following morning had seen such fun and games for all! Frank Taylor had never seen so many folk in his pub before. He was to tell us all later.

"I hope I've enough ale 'int' cellar." Frank had said all worried like! A loud outburst of laughter followed his comment and this was when old Frank began to look even more concerned. A rare sight from him this.

"'Thy Alright', Frank." I asked as I made my way over to the Tap Room Bar. I was still wearing my green keeper's top and kit as well as my football boots! The one's I had worn constantly for the past ten year's including that glorious 1966 World Cup Victory! I chose though that night to place these into the Charity Auction which was all a part of the Charity fund raising that day.

"Need a hand, Frank?" I called out.

"'Newer', lad, you're aireight! But I might have to ask your 'Charly' to 'muck' in later." Charlotte always told Frank she wasn't a 'Charly'. She didn't take this as one of the Big Man's jokes but the funny thing was that Frank had never actually called her this nickname to her face but only when he was asking someone else if she was OK or asking if she might help him out or do him a favour. Usually if the pub was busy.

By the time Frank had locked up the Shakespeare Tavern in the Valley in the early hours of May 13 1971 he was exhausted! He was so happy and relieved too but nevertheless he was shattered! The relief came about when he didn't run out of beer, spirits and soft drinks for folks after all that

Charity Night in the 'Shakey' had flown by. One minute I'd looked up at the pub clock which read 10.00 p.m. and before I knew, 2.00 a.m. had dawned! A lot had happened that night. So much money had been raised and lots of fun had by all. Players shirts and other kit along with signed footballs. All these by the 1966 World Cup winning squad. Also auctioned were match day tickets from the finals including the final of the 29 June 1966. Frank had done such a wonderful job in organising the event. Snooker, Darts and other pub games were also a big hit but the highlight of the night came just after midnight!

"Thank you ever so much for supporting all the kids at the Hospital, folks." Mick was up on the microphone to say a few words but these were lost by him. His piece of paper on which he had jotted down a few notes falling from his hands!

"Sorry, folks. I'm just so made up that you all came along here tonight." Mick said with great feeling. He then just couldn't find the words to express how grateful he was. He found a place to rest! Sitting in the very same seat from the night when he had announced the Charity Day a year or so before!

'Big Frank's Quiz' had been a regular Wednesday night event but he had called this 'Big Frank's Charity Quiz' for this occasion. Frank was looking a little weary as he had played a big part in the day and now the night's organisation. Not just in taking time out to see that that the Charity Day at Linden Park went well. He had been superb all the year around helping with the fund raising and all!

The Quiz was a great success. Laughter and cheers filling both the lounge and Tap Room of the 'Shakey'. There were 20 general knowledge questions. I was expecting Rachel's team to win once again. She being a regular quizzer on a Wednesday night. But the big surprise of the whole day came when 'Mick's Marvels' became the first of 'Big Frank's Charity Night' winners along with Charlotte, Mick and Aimee Joyce. I was asked to accept the trophy of 'Big Frank's Tankard'. A prize we held for the next 12 months!

The Charity Day and night time in the pub finally came to an end. We had raised a lot of money for the Sheffield Children's Hospital and we'd had such a celebration and so much joy along the way!!!

The following year Charlotte invited two dear old friends of ours to stay with us. We had an emotional time as we met up with them both at Sheffield Train Station.

"Mary! Mary! Can I let go of you now, please?" Charlotte asked as Mary Omalley's tears streamed down her face!

"Oh, girl you're both like the son and daughter were never blessed with." Mary told us as we settled down back home at Steel Road.

Jim was looking frail at this time but was full of joy and telling us all his Brighton news. Mary and Jim were settled and happy since their move to retire there some year's before.

"Oh God, lad! I've been telling the whole of Brighton about how you helped out in winning that little tournament against Brazil a couple of years ago!" Jim's eyes dazzled as he patted me on my back several times. He had curious coloured eyes! Kind of bluey-grey. I'd never seen such a mix before. James's hair had now become sensible. Gone was his quiff from that first time we'd met. He now was greying and thinning and combing his hair back to his scalp.

Mary's hair was still a vivid amber but of a paler shade now. She was very emotional for the fortnight she stayed with us. Thinking nothing of this at first but Charlotte told me that Mary had confided in her. We were all going up to Manchester and the night before Charlotte told me some eye-opening news about James and Mary Omalley. I was quiet the next day as we all travelled to Manchester. Trying to get my head around this revelation while we were on the train out of Sheffield Charlotte asked.

"You're quiet, Mt Minton. What's on your mind, love?" We then both went along to the train's buffet bar for some tea and snacks whilst Jim and Mary stayed in their seats in the carriage.

"I've been trying to work out this marriage thing," I said as I clamoured to find the right words as to what I wanted to say to her.

"Are you sure you're OK, Gary?" she asked me again.

"What wedding thing? I don't know what you mean, love," Charlotte then asked. My nerves then brought my laughter as I adjusted my suit's clothing. We had all put on our 'Glad Rags' for our visit to the Omalley's family up in Manchester. We sat there in the buffet bar in silence for a while!

"So, old James is not married to Mary then. 'Allus' thought they were wed! Didn't you, love?" I then asked as the awful quiet began to grate. Charlotte was looking all washed out and pale! Her jet-black hair was not as neat and well kempt as usual. She sipped away at her cup of tea before gently nodding her head.

"Yeah, Gaz. Yeah, I know." Charlotte said after what seemed a lifetime in her very weary, tired way. I decided then to drop the Omalley 'married or not' topic.

"Well!" Charlotte then suddenly said.

"When you and Jim were chatting in our living room yesterday. Mary looked troubled. So I asked if she had anything on her mind? Kind of thing."

"Yeah, go on Charlotte." I said calmly.

"Well, Mrs 'O' then suddenly burst into tears. Just like she did when we met them at the Station, off the train, Gary. Oh Gary! I just didn't know what the bloody hell to do then! The poor woman! I just couldn't find any words to comfort her. "Also she was clinging on to me again for all she was worth! I started to well up with the tears myself then, Gaz, to be honest. Then she suddenly lets go of me and blurts it all out! All about when she and Jim had left Belfast as teenagers because they had a big fall out with their families. Apparently James is a Catholic and Mary's Protestant and this had caused all kinds of bother. They had both fled Ireland and settled in London for all those year's but now they have built bridges again with their elderly parent's. So this is why they now want to go to Manchester. So we presumed they were married, Gary," Charlotte said. "They haven't seen Elsie and George for such a long time now!"

"Whose?" I interrupted before Charlotte laughed.

Then gently reminded me to 'Keep up, Gary'. Then explained more of the 'Omalley Mystery'.

"Elsie and George Sheridan are Mrs 'O's' folks." Charlotte said.

"Are you OK, love? You look worn out!" I asked of Charlotte after she'd told me that Mary and Jim were going to Manchester to get married! Having called to see us both at the same time. They also had to decide to tie the knot. They also asked something we were more than delighted to do for them.

Once we had agreed to witness the marriage of Mr James and Mrs Mary Omalley the tension subsided somewhat.

Then Mary suggested we all celebrate! So Jim said we should try to find a suitable pub.

We only had a couple of drinks in a 'Boozer' called 'The Red Witch'. One of those places which was very much a local's place. The Landlord was friendly enough but as for the customer'

As they eyed us with suspicion. Whispers and sly looks were not a welcome for us, so we decided to leave there.

James was looking so smart. He was wearing a black pin striped suit along with a waistcoat of emerald green. This was a shiny material. Oh, so 'snazzy!' He also had his little emerald green handkerchief peeping out of his suit jacket pocket. When he had walked Mary up to the entrance of the nursing home, both of them hand in hand Mary stopped stand still. She looked lovingly at James before straightening his cream-coloured tie and tickling his emerald handkerchief in his pocket. She then said,

"You'll do for me, Jimbo! Now don't go showing me up 'nay'. Do you hear? Remember Manners, young man, and speak when you're spoken to." Mary then winked and chuckled with James.

Once Mary had relaxed, she inspected her 'to be' new husband. She checked Jim's appearance just as if he were to meet the Queen herself. Her giddy, nervous energy and worries of the past few days had passed. taking off her wide brimmed, sunny-yellow hat, she then made sure she was looking immaculate for the big occasion. Finally making sure her red carnation was attached to her hat!

Mr and Mrs Sheridan had been residents in the Nursing Home on the outskirts of Manchester for five year's. Both now in their dotage, yet they were still very bright and cheerful. But their physical infirmity meant they rarely left the home. I walked around the lovely grounds of the Nursing Home. The gardens were really great and well kept. We didn't want to intrude on the reunion between Jim, Mary and her parent's. Charlotte believed that the reunion could be awkward for them all after 20 years or more had passed. The way things had happened in that Jim and Mary had just left home for London and also the religious reason's was a sensitive issue!

By the New Year celebrations to welcome in 1977 meant life had been sweet and sour again. Charlotte had a new and exciting job. One she had settled to very well. Renewing her friendship with Tara Bailey. Back in 1974, Charlotte had taken on the role of Art Treasurer at Wiseman Museum. This was next to the City Library in Sheffield. There was a lot of responsibility involved with this position.

The annual Charity Fun Day had gone from strength to strength. I suggested an exhibition. I had begun to enjoy photography. This hobby led me, with the help of Mick and Evie, to take a variety of photographs of Steelsbridge. Then room's had become available at the library. So I asked and then was given permission to hold an exhibition. So in early 1977, we spruced up the room's in the basement of the library. In our spare time I helped Evie and Mick to paint and decorate and then display the photographs of the Valley.

By 1978 the photo exhibition had been very popular. We had appealed the folk to bring in any photographs they may have had. So along with Mick I gathered together some impressive ones – photos which showed Steelsbridge and her people dating back to the first World War. Then we displayed these and blended them with one's since the Great War.

Steelsbridge town had grown from a rural environment of fields and farms into factories and mills in the 1920s. When communities had flourished on housing estate's throughout the town! A Library and Town Hall came along and then much later, of course, the Football Club. Steelsbridge Town A.F.C came into existence in the spring of 1946.

By the close of the 1974/75 football season, I was 34 years of age. That previous season had been a disaster! So much so that Charlotte and Alice Burroughs ended up talking Jack out of handing in his resignation. Our club had come within just a point of dropping down into Division 2. I had been given the arm band to be Captain during this season of woe!

1976 was the hottest summer I have ever known! Otherwise life was pretty mundane. By the height of that summer stand pipes were installed at the end of every road in the Valley!

The Charity Fun day of the glorious summer of 1976 was again our highlight of the year. Also a dear old friend came back to help us out but I was really concerned about him!

Apart from the regular training sessions at 'Steels' I also chose to do weekly exercise of my own. A couple of times a week I would go jogging or walking up to Smithsly Village and back. Sometimes a fast walk up there and other times I would break into sprinting or just jog along. One day whilst doing this I heard my name being shouted out!

"Gary! Gary, lad! How are you?"

Looking around and having come to a standstill I looked across the wide Church Road to see a man I just didn't recognise at all. *Some old school pal?* I thought. *Maybe someone from the football club even?* As this tall, long-haired figure approached me, I was still not the wiser. The stranger was scruffy looking, not exactly overweight but he did have a paunch of a stomach! I was just about to dash off into another sprint when the penny suddenly dropped just like a dull ache in my heart!!

"Sammy! Sammy, me old. Is that you, lad? God, are you OK? You don't look too clever, lad. If you don't mind me saying! Come on why don't we go back to 'yours' for a bit?" Although Sammy was trying to show a cheery face. I just knew he wasn't himself. Sam had always been sensitive and a worrier but what shocked me the most was Sam's appearance!! I had never seen Sammy with so much as a hair on his head out of place, always keeping his 12 stone in weight. Also what was sad was the state of his clothes! They were filthy and his shoes were 'holy!' That is they were ripped and battered.

Sammy's folks looked worried sick! They were smashing people but I just couldn't help but notice a very strange atmosphere in their home. A brittle atmosphere when I was asked in by Tony and Amanda.

"I'm 'gonna' have to go to bed. Sorry, Gaz. I will only have an hour." Is all Sam said as he walked down the hallway to his bedroom. I knew for definite then that things were not right.

Tony and Amanda's Cottage was very homely. Not at all showy but comfortable. They showed me into their living room with every wall space lined with books. There was a bright wine carpet with flecks of cream flowers. A soft cream suit of a plush sofa and two armchair's. Amanda was so pretty with golden hair falling almost to her waist. Very slim and wearing corduroy trousers with a bright yellow silk blouse. But I hadn't seen her so drawn and washed out before. Her eyes reddened as if tears had been shed. Tony wasn't his usual chatty self either. Being a lot quieter than I remember. They made me a cup of tea and then both sat on the sofa, holding hands.

"We are so worried about Samuel, Gary. We have always worked problems out as a family haven't, darling?"

Amanda said as Tony sipped away at his tea from a China cup before simply replying.

"I know love, I know love." He said as he squeezed his wife's hand.

"Please, if there is anything…is there any help I can give you? I was so…sor…sorry when I noticed you, Sam. I mean…sorry, Amanda…Tony." Amanda then began to weep as if the years of heartache was leaving her! She then began to cling on to Tony, who also shed a small tear.

"Oh, dear God, Gary, I'm so sorry. I'm so embarrassed!" Amanda added as she began to wipe away the salty tears before composing herself once again!

"Please, don't be sorry, Amanda. Seems to me that has just done you the world of good!" I managed to say. Tony then burst out laughing and I joined in with doing the same!

By the final days of 1978 Sammy was very much back to rude health. The recovery had been slow. Amanda and Tony told me some eye-opening facts! Sammy had suffered from severe bouts of depression since his early 20s. The year's he spent in Australia and London had been a tremendous time!

He did have episodes of being depressed abroad but on the whole he had lived a full and happy life living away.

"The problems seem to have been when he returned to London. When he decided to begin writing." Amanda had explained to me one night at their Cottage.

Since the mid-60s Sammy had been in regular contact with his Mum and Dad. Always telling them he was fine and that he had many friends and he was going out regularly in London.

"But, Gary lad," Tony continued to explain.

"He was living in his flat in London and rarely left the place. He was working hard on his writing for the newspapers, magazines and had a book on the go but really he wasn't 'seeing a soul'."

The meltdown of Sammy came when he returned home to the Valley. The day I came across him on the Church Road proved to be a real blessing in disguise!

We were sat in a quiet corner. I was staring at the wine sodden note. The Shakespeare was deserted. I took a long gulp from my pint before demolishing the half bottle of Southern Comfort.

"Oreight, Gaz, lad. Time I hit the sack, lad. It's midnight kid." In the weeks and months that followed, I remember very little apart from those words of 'Big Frank'. Of him asking if I was OK and of the blurry scrawl of Charlotte's beautifully written note. Why I still have this note I just don't know?

I will remember that freezing cold December night of 1981 in the 'Shakey' for such a long time! For the next two years, I endured some very dark, titanic days in my young life!

Days after my long marriage to Charlotte Manners had fallen to pieces.

Looking back now our problems seem to have started because of money. But this was not the real reason for our separating. The animosity between us had come to light many year's before. On reflection our honeymoon with the Omalley's back in the autumn of 1961 was the start of all of it. We were so happy though back then but all those years later when I found myself in London's St Thomas's Hospital I had time to reflect!

In the New Year of 1982 I recalled a blazing row – one which the subject of was to resurface over and over again of our next 20 years together. I remember one day on our honeymoon we had returned from a lovely day out in London and Charlotte was sat with Mary Omalley in the Hotel kitchen. I was feeling knackered so I went off to our room for a 'kip' for a couple of hours. When I woke up, Charlotte was downstairs. The room was cold and bleak.

"You OK, love?" I remember Charlotte asking once I had washed and got myself all ready for the evening meal. But the shrugs and silent treatment along with the occasional sigh when I told her I was fine wasn't a good sign. Once we had eaten in the Hotel dining room, Charlotte flew at me once we had got back to our room!

She was still so upset the following morning. I was shell shocked. Her harsh and heartless words the previous evening had been a real bombshell to me! We were fine and enjoyed the rest of the holiday but the fact that Charlotte wanted a child was the big problem between us then. Over the years to follow. Our marriage was shadowed by this! Her pent-up anger and frustration from time to time leaving me in bits as far as my emotions went. These feelings between us were never resolved though. We would fight and then the remorse calmed us. But a year or a few months later, we'd have another shouting match and then make up! This vicious circle of bad feeling between us both ground me down eventually. But the baby or rather us not having one was always there between myself and Charlotte!

By the spring of 1983 I had turned a corner! I was finally off the booze and determined to continue with my football career with 'Steels'. But where I got my sense of being able to fight for a brighter future was when Charlotte gave me the news I had been dreaming of all my life. By the time I had worked to be fully fit the prospect of finally being a father made my life wonderful!

I had asked to see Charlotte once Jack Burroughs had brought me back home from London and when I had spent some time in the 'Sunshine Woods' clinic, there I spoke with Charlotte on the phone for hours some days. We both finally came to accept that we had been ignoring the 'Baby' or lack of one for too many years and had been hurting each other. Then trying to mend this hurt between us far too many times. I accepted that I would never go back to Charlotte. We were to look forward to being new parent's however!

To have the child we had both yearned for. To give the kid everything he or she would now need and so want for nothing. But we both knew at the same time that we could only ever remain friends in the future.

"Minton, what's bloody well up 'wi ye', lad? Come on, Gaz, listen up." Those words from Jack Burroughs's on the eve of the 1983. F.A. Cup Semi Final were my wakeup call!

Manchester Town were waiting for us. The only hurdle between 'Steels' and our first ever F.A. Cup Final at the famous Wembley Stadium in London on the 12th May 1983 on what was a glorious, hot and sunny day!

The two set of supporters were in fine voice! Both standing together, giving the stadium a multi-coloured sea of blue, yellow, red, white and black! The Wembley pitch was superb that day! The lush green grass was ideal for making the football fizz across the turf. I was feeling confident. I had lost weight and I was the fittest I could remember being in a long time. At 43 year's old I was just like a kid again! I leapt and caught the ball and was up for saving everything that came my way! I just didn't want the ref to blow for the end of the first half. We were expecting a harsh response from the boss at half time but he was quite the opposite. You didn't know sometimes how Jack was going to react?

This time he was calmness itself and heaped his praise on us! Our defence had been solid and I was quietly taken aside just before we came back out for the second half.

"You're playing a blinder, kid. 'Ye' really are! Just keep on doing what 'ye' are doing," Jack said to me and then winked. He was looking weary though and we all so much wanted to bring him the silverware he so deserved!

The second 45 minutes was so different! Our opponents weakened. They began to look spent! Giving the ball away all the time! In the 67th minute I took a goal kick. The ball was nodded on from the halfway line. A fine pass then found our young centre forward Noel Lawton. I watched as the local 'Steels' lad turned and arched the ball into the top right-hand corner of the net!! Noel. A slight, blonde-haired lad. His yellow and blue shirt baggy. His shorts of blue. Ill-fitting was mobbed by us all! A scrum of lemon-yellow, Navy-blue and a solitary green keepers jersey and shorts!

Manchester Town were out on their feet when we scored!

They just couldn't live with us in that second half!

To say my emotions were tested following the ref's final whistle at Villa Road would be more than true. I was so overjoyed and jubilant!! I didn't have Champagne or any booze. I just wanted to savour every single moment of what I knew all too well was one of my last appearance for 'Steels'! But I was given the shock of all my days by 10.00 p.m. that night! The phone call I received from the Hospital was such a sobering one!

Charlotte had been rushed into the Sheffield Northern Hospital that afternoon! I had been told during our celebrations at Villa Road that she was very poorly indeed and I needed to come back to Sheffield at once!

By midnight, Alice Burroughs had driven me back up north. I think Alice was the only one at the Semi Final who had also not touched a drop of alcohol.

"I will drop you off at the Hospital, Gary love and then I will be at home. Phone me at any time if you need anything at all, love. Don't worry, I'm sure Charlotte and the baby will be fine. It's just a precaution. They need to take care to make sure they are both healthy and well." Alice was lovely. Her comforting words did lift me out the doldrums. But my mood descended again once I was on the maternity ward!

At 2.00 a.m. on 13 May 1983 I was stood looking down at the love of my life! Charlotte lay on a Hospital bed in the Chapel. She looked so at peace. Her raven long hair as beautiful and neat as always. But I was consumed by regret as soon as I returned to the home of Jack and Alice Burroughs. I thought that seeing Charlotte's body would be something I was able to handle but once they had told me we had lost our child also. I just could not stand to be in my own skin! The guilt, the heartache, regret and sorrow. All began to swim through my body like a surgeon's knife!

Chapter 13

By my 45th birthday I had come to terms with lots of things in my life. Between losing Charlotte and baby Florence in the May of 1983 and summer of 1985 life was a struggle but did get sweeter!

Charlotte had passed away on 13 May 1983. We had already decided our baby girl's name. We were to have named her Florence. A name we had both agreed upon because of all the love and affection we had always held for Mrs Flora Palmer – the lovely 'Mrs P'.

By the ending of May 1983 we had said our goodbye's to Charlotte. The funeral was modest. I was still reeling from losing her! Still numb at never going to be a father.

The sun shone brightly upon St Pauls Church! The one set within the village of Smithsly. Myself, Mick and Rachel attended the service, of course. For what was a simple memorial for Florence and Charlotte. Both now rest together in a simple, sweet grave in St Paul's cemetery.

Alice Burroughs's organised a small 'Do' following the funeral but this did not go well because I wished myself miles away again from 'The Shakespeare Tavern' and Steelsbridge altogether after what turned out to be a complete disaster of an afternoon!!

Jack and Alice Burroughs were so pissed when I arrived at the 'Shakey' for the wake! I had decided to walk down the mile or so from Smithsly Village after the funeral with both Rachel and Mick. We arrived at the pub just shy of 1.00 p.m. Charlotte had mentioned to me once that if she were to leave this world, she didn't want folk to make a fuss at her funeral. She said she'd like a simple service with happy songs and uplifting hymns with no one wearing black but to dress in bright colours.

"I don't want the word 'mourners' mentioned either, Gary love," Was something else Charlotte told me. I recall this conversation clearly from the time we were on the train back from London following our fantastic honeymoon! We were both exhausted and slept for most of the journey back from there.

A couple of years before we buried Charlotte, I remember Rachel had bought a sunshine yellow dress – one Charlotte had bought for her as a birthday present. Mick looked very smart. He wore a gold shirt and a crimson pin striped three-piece suit. He also had a bright yellow daffodil, neatly pinned to the lapel of his suit. This had been Charlotte's favourite flower. For my sweetheart's funeral, I chose a suit and waistcoat of sky blue with a lemon shirt. I wore my beloved Steel's tie. The one Charlotte had gifted to me when I had won the 1966 World Cup with England. A tie of Navy blue and yellow with the crest of both Steelsbridge Town and England proudly embroidered in the centre.

We had walked out of St Pauls Church in Smithsly Village with two songs that meant the world to Charlotte playing.

Ain't Got No! I Got Life by Nina Simon and the *Beatles*

'She Loves You'. Both of which were rarely heard to be off the juke box in the 'Shakey' or at our home at 'Steel Road'.

I came to adore these songs too since I had first began courting Charlotte.

As soon as we walked into the Shakespeare pub, I just knew something was up. The atmosphere was ice cold! There were raised voices and we heard Frank trying to keep the peace and stop the situation from boiling over. I said to Mick and Rachel that we best go off into the lounge side of the pub. I would try my best to get served for us in there.

"I'll get the drinks in Rachel and then let Mick know when he comes out of the bog and before he goes off into the Tap Room that we are in here. Well, until whatever is kicking off next door calm's down anyhow. But Mick had already made his way into the other side!"

Over by the big juke box and in one of the booths, Jack Burroughs and his wife Alice had come to blows!! So much so that Frank Taylor had to get in amongst everyone and take action. 'Big Frank' marched on over to Jack and Alice. Jack was stood sodden wet from having a full pint that his wife had showered over him. Old Jack had then thrown off his jacket on to a nearby seat before tightly clenching both his fists, just as he was about to throw a hefty left hook at Alice Burroughs, Frank stepped on in there. Jack staggered away from everyone's grasp and then bawled out.

"You 'Fecking' Bitch!!! What the 'FULK' is that for bloody for? You Crazy Bitch!" Jack was absolutely legless! Another new one on me where old Jack was concerned but what was to happen next was to almost cause a bar room brawl!! Even though Frank had already separated the Burroughs's couple. Jack was leaning on the juke box while his Alice was in floods of tears as she sat in one of the booths just over by the Tap Room Bar area.

"For FULKS sake!!!" I hollered out at the top of my voice! I then turned to Mick and Rachel to ask.

"What the bloody hell has got into those two? I have never ever seen old Jack pissed. As for Alice I thought she never went near the stuff!" I just couldn't fathom what was going on. This was just 'Barmy' behaviour!

"Fulk knows?! Come on, Mick, Gaz! Let's bloody well go home. I've just about Fulking had enough of today." This was another shock to my system. In all the many year's I had known Rachel Greaves I'd never heard her swear, lose her composure or say anything negative at all. But Charlotte's passing had certainly brought out the worst in all of us that day!

"OK, forget those drinks." I ended up saying and we all got out of the 'Shakey' as fast as we knew how!

"That kid of Charlotte's was that miserable Scottish Bastards!!" We could all three of us hear Alice Burroughs's screaming at the top of her lungs as we left the pub!!!

When this sank in I could have destroyed Frank's Boozer!! The football ground and set up dynamite to blow the whole of that God forsaken Town to Kingdom Come!! I sat on the wall outside the 'Shakey'. My legs havin gone to sleep. I could feel the blood draining from my face and body and I just wanted to SCREAM!!!

I just couldn't stand Steelsbridge any longer! The morning following Charlotte's wake I asked Mick if he fancied coming to London with me? He was in a similar state of mind. Only too pleased to drive us both down the M1! We had both been suffocated by the place. "Home!" They say. "Is Where the Heart Is." but sometimes you wish yourself 'bloody' miles and miles away!

We only intended staying for a couple of weeks! Mick had always been so welcome at his Aunt Maureen's in Clapham, South London. Her husband Robert was a really easy going bloke and I think he welcomed some male company? What was only at first going to be a little rest bite for me anyway to be able to sort my head out turned into an opportunity to reflect and rebuild my life! The astonishing news that Jack Burroughs was the father of Charlotte's child was to be a blessing in the end by developing into a fine few months of work, friendship and getting to be close mates again for Mick and 'Yours Truly'. 'Everything Works Out'. No matter what…this was something I believed to be true!

After a while spent in Clapham I was dreading returning to the Valley! Those first few days with Maureen and Rob were such a pleasure! A real release from gossip and the nasty spiteful atmosphere of home.

Between the May and Christmas of 1983 I was too busy to dwell on my recent past! Mick was a lot more relaxed and happier. The days were hot and Robert asked if Mick could do a job for him. I helped out too and a month from our arrival in South London the back garden of Mick's aunt was looking fine. Mick dealt with all the hedges and nettles. The overgrown grass and trees whilst I raked and gathered all that Michael had cut down. We both had a great time working on something that we thought we knew nothing of in gardening.

Robert and Maureen lived at what they lovingly called 'The Homestead'. A name they both thought suited their large house. An impressive Georgian property with four bedrooms! They lived a simple life. They had only a few refined pieces of furniture. A cooker, fridge and washing machine.

Mick and I were suited to having been given the back bedroom as guests. We were so grateful for Rob and Maureen's kindness!

One day Rob was stood at the large bay window's in the living room.

"That bloody garden is like a jungle, love." Robert observed with a long sigh.

"Well, you staring at the thing all morning won't make the grass, not grow!" Maureen said as she smiled and winked at Mick and then me. Suddenly Mick jumped up from the Sofa and nodded to me. We both then shuffled over to stand with Robert. Being like a bit of a fun double act. We were warmed then by the sun that blazed through the bay window's!

"Do you need a hand with that jungle out there, young Robert?" Mick asked in his cheeky, boyish way as he gently nudged me in the ribs.

"Yeah, Rob, we could both make ourselves useful while we are staying here. Have you any gardening tools or whatever mate?" I suddenly got excited as I offered this with Mick and really warmed to the idea.

"Oh…no…lad's! Listen I wasn't hinting or suggesting in anyway. I was just commenting just saying lad's, that's all."

Robert had exceptional manners and a heart of gold from a well to do family. When I'd first met him I got him all wrong! Thinking him a bit of a toff and snooty but that soon passed and we got along famously from then on!

"Oh, for heaven's sake, Rob. The lads are offering to help us out. Stop wittling and worrying about life". "Let them help! We can all pitch in." As soon as Maureen had got these words said we were all down in 'The Homesteads' huge garden amongst the tall grass, nettles, weeds and overgrown greenery.

Eventually we came to the foot of the garden. There stood a browny-green weather beaten shed. The paint had peeled away long since. Giving way to bare and in some places, rotting wood!

By the time the sun had begun to set over Clapham that Sunday evening the garden of 'The Homestead' had begun to take on a whole new life! We had all got stuck in! Robert with the shears hacking away at the hedges which were high and surrounded the garden an all sides. I came across a rusty old scythe. This didn't take long to sharpen up. This then made short work of tall grasses and the nettles. Meanwhile Mick and Maureen chopped away at the tree branches with a sharp axe we also discovered in the old shed.

The following morning Maureen and Robert were up bright and early. At 7.00 a.m. both worked long hours in the City of London. So having made headway in their vast garden the previous day both myself and Mick carried on! I trimmed all the privet hedges whilst Mick tackled the long grasses, nettles and all.

What I remember most of all about that particular summer in Clapham was the blazing hot sunshine! Everyday seemed to be drenched in sunlight. After a fortnight we had broken the back of the garden for everything to look, well, like a garden! We discussed Robert being able to bring some much-needed colour to his garden and grow vegetables. So over that summertime along with Rob and Maureen's neighbours we made great improvements! Their next-door neighbour Mickey was a great help! Giving us a much-needed hand in going in his builder's van to the local garden centre. Trial and error was our way rather an immense amount of error and laughter including a time when Mick thought some fine red roses would brighten up the centre of the garden. But his patience for seeing them bloom in all their glory got the better of him! He then dug up these young rose plants before ending up then digging up most of the garden!

"Gardens don't just flourish just like that, Mick mate!" I reminded him.

"'Tha' has to wait for the veg and flowers to grow and blossom. It all takes time lad." I added.

"Oh, so sorry, Mr Percy Thrower!" Mick replied laughing and then tossing his floppy white sun hat at me!

By mid-November of 1983 Mick was beginning to think seriously of staying down in London. I was thinking along the same lines! I didn't think I had all that much to go back to Sheffield for. Steelsbridge was my home and I loved her for all she was and had inflicted upon me, but my footballing career had long since been done with. My personal life was badly in need of rebuilding. I gave a lot of thought to what had happened with Charlotte and the baby. The gardening had been a wonderful tonic! Chatting with Mick, Maureen and Robert helped me be thankful for all the great times I'd had over the years in football and of course with Charlotte! All the blessings in my life far outweighed the painful times!

Not only did we transform Maureen and Robert's garden's but we also got stuck into the neighbours too! Some of these only needed a bit of a tidy whilst others were in need of the same kind of work we had given to Rob and Maureen's! Rob did insist on paying us fairly for our efforts on his garden's and the word-of-mouth effect on their neighbours meant both Mick and I managed to save up a nice bit of cash that summer!

By mid-November of 1983 we had both decided to travel on back to Sheffield! This was after Mick received a phone call – one in which we knew we just could not ignore!

"The 'Doc' says old Jack tumbled over in all the ice and snow 'Gaz'!" Mick said as we made our way to Jack Burroughs's Hospital room.

"Hit his head or 'sumat!'. Apparently they've had bad weather here lately," Mick also told me.

I've never been able to abide Hospitals. The white of all the walls and stench of poorly folk! I had been in the Northern Royal a few times. Visiting folk I knew wasn't all that bad but the boredom of staying on a ward as a patient just drove me 'barmy'!.

Fortunately we found Jack was in his own room as we arrived at the Royal. This was all part of a main ward but there were three annexed single rooms. One of which Jack was. I have to say I got quite a jolt when I walked in there! Jack was ashen faced! He also had a deep purple bruise around his nose and left eye. Along with a thick wad of bandages around his forehead. He was sleeping as we entered his room but began to come too as Mick took a look at the clip board which was hooked on to the foot of his bed! This recorded the tests that had been taken by the doctor and nurses caring for old Jack.

"Hey Up, Big Man." Mick said quietly as I sat nervous and unsure of what to do in a large floral armchair which was placed next to Jack's Hospital bed!

We stayed for about 45 minutes with Jack. He kept drifting in and out of sleep in the time we were there. In fact I don't think he was with it at all! After leaving him some books and fruit along with a few newspapers, we let the nursing staff attend to him.

"Shit, Mick, I wasn't expecting 'told', lad to be, so you know?" I said as we strolled back down the wide, clinical and clean corridors of The Royal.

"I know, Gaz, lad. Me neither. Must have bashed his 'sen' up good and proper when he fell!"

By the Christmas of 1983 I was willing the New Year to arrive! 1983 had been the worst! I couldn't wait to put all the shit behind me! I was so thankful to Mick though! That summer in London. The gardening had been such break for us both. We had sorted our heads out! This had made all the difference to me in particular.

I returned to Steelsbridge refreshed and fitter than I had been in year's!

The end

Epilogue

By the close of the 1984/85 football season, Gary Minton was a few months shy of his 45th birthday. He knew then that the time had arrived! He realised that the time had come to finally finish his football career!

Gary intended to retire quietly. He had the intent of giving Steelsbridge Town his very best. Playing one last season at Linden Park. As his legs had been betraying him once too often. The arthritis and cramps were no longer easy to ignore. But there were events happening behind the scenes at 'Steels' which would give Gary the greatest night since his 1966 World Cup triumph as England No 1! A night that would hold wonderful memories of how much the fans, management and Steelsbridge itself adored their local hero! Gary never had a clue about his big send off! Once the final match of the 84/85 season was over all he had on his mind was a well-deserved holiday.

As Gary joined the rest of the team for a traditional end of season lap of honour of the Linden Park ground his life-long friend, Michael Joyce was in deep conversation up in the main stand! Along with Jack and Alice Burroughs, Mick was fine tuning a very special testimonial for the most successful and longest serving footballer at Steelsbridge Town!

On a hot July evening in 1985, the stands and every available space was taken at the Linden Park Stadium! The young, elderly and all those with deep affection for Gary Paul Minton were there!

The first Gary knew of this special match in his honour was when he was asked to come down to Linden Park on the 6th of July 1985. Mick had told Gary he had been invited to open a new bar and Hospitality suite at the ground!

"There's a lot of bloody folk here, Mick, 'int' there? Just for a bit of a ceremony to open a bar or whatever it is? Isn't there, mate?" Gary asked as they both headed for the players entrance which overlooked the club car park.

"Oh, 'tha' knows what folk are like Gary lad. 'Out' for a free 'nosh' up and some cheap 'fizz'." But Mick's attempt to smother a huge grin with his blue and yellow 'Steels' scarf gave the game away! He began to giggle and couldn't hold the secret any longer!

The floodlights were shining bright! The stands were absolutely packed out with folk! Kids and fans of all ages were even spilling out on to the Linden Park pitch from all four sides with supporters singing and stamping their feet on the floor of the wooden stands!

The atmosphere was electric! The 'Steels' faithful also threw up lemon and blue 'Ticker Tape'!. The same coloured balloons were released into the warm night air from the centre circle just prior to kick off. Gary was moved so much, in particular by the Steelsbridge Brass Band who played their hearts out as they led out the two teams!

Once Gary Minton had got his head around what this occasion meant, he could finally relax and enjoy his match!

He was so overjoyed to meet and shake warmly by the hand – players he hadn't clapped eyes upon in many a year!

Gary took his place where he was most at home. Between the goalposts. He was honoured to be made Captain for the first time in a 'Steels' green keepers jersey. Captain of the 'Steelsbridge Town All Stars'. The team included his best pal Michael Joyce as well as some of the current 'Steels' lad's. One or two had come out of retirement for Gary.

Players, who had been regular for 'Town' back when their guest of honour was only starting out for his home town club and just making his mark in the game! The 'All Stars' opponents for Gary's special night were a stellar side! A collection of players, even 20 years on from lifting the World Cup were still able to shine. Simon Clifton was in goal. The defence of Arthur Harvey. Captain Bobby Giles and Johnny Wright at left back. Frank Warner, Jimmy Gold and Len Fleet made up this nostalgic midfield. Tommy Sharpe and Roy Goldman led the front line. The player, who Gary Minton was most delighted to see, turn out for him was only 17 years of age during the World Cup summer of 1966. Frank Haley had been an outstanding player for Leeds Town. Although Frank Haley was tipped by many in the game to be in the 1966 England World Cup Squad, he didn't quite make it but never the less he did go on to be one of the greatest England forwards of his generation!

As Gary hears the referee's shrill whistle to begin, his mind began to go back. In flashbacks all the years of 'Steels' came flooding back. Then all those England matches – a replay of his whole footballing life was being played out in his head. This scared the shit out of him for a short time but as he composed himself and he began to relax, he loved every single minute of his big night just like that teenager who had signed for 'Steels' all those many year's before. Gary Minton played with all the free spirit he possessed.

Throughout the first half, there was a lot of fun to be had! There was a lot of exhibition play! After just 15 minutes of the first half, Gary himself instead of handling the ball from a pass back from Mick Joyce, chose to dribble through not only the 1966 World Cup lad's but also his own 'Steels' team mates as well! Comical, imitation tackles and his old England mate, Simon Clifton, diving the wrong way for Gary then to smash the ball high into the net! This brought the ear splitting and jubilant noise from everybody in the stadium!!

Gary was in sensational form on his testimonial night! He saved genuine hard shot's from the England World Cup lad's. Top corner, bottom corner, left, right of him. Gary just dealt with anything thrown his way! His trademark bravery of diving at the opponent's feet and claiming the football was still there. Diving headlong, all around his penalty area and claiming the ball out of the night air. Gary was at his very best! That orange Casey football didn't stand a chance against Mr G Minton!

The match officials for the memorable 'Gary Minton Testimonial of 1985 were well-known to all in the town of Steelsbridge. By now, 56-year-old Jack Burroughs was given the role as match referee. Although he didn't venture much further than the centre circle. He was often heard to shout out, "Just Shut, Ye Rattle" and "I may 'nay' be able to run anymore but there 'nay' wrong 'wi' me eyesight! So let's be 'getting' on 'wi' it, 'ye' lot." This was all good humoured banter and added nicely to the event!

As the two teams, referee and linesmen came out on to the Linden Park pitch, long applause and loud cheering greeted them all! The lines were being run by the town's jovial and popular Landlord. One Mr Frank Turner. This special match for Gary had fallen nicely on Frank's 60th birthday!

With a 'Steels' Navy blue and lemon giant shirt and baggy tracksuit bottoms. 'Big Frank' stood to wave to all four sides of the Stadium with a woodbine dangling from his lips! Frank then waved his bright red linesman's flag high above his head! A more serious attitude was however taken by the other person running the line. A professional looking Aimee Joyce was now 29! She was wearing a striking yellow shirt, black shorts and yellow socks with a cute black trim. She was immaculate! She wanted to do this as a thank you for the kindness and support given by her home town club over the year's!

Confusion and amusement for everyone came with just ten minutes left of the first half with Jack Burroughs's managing to plod on up to the goalmouth. He is then seen to be having a long conversation with the star player of the night, Mr Gary Minton booing and stamping on the boards of the stand's leads to the 'ref' searching in his knee length, black overcoat pockets. He then finds first of all a luminous yellow card! Swiftly, then followed by the ominous red! Jack then gives an almighty blast on his whistle before them pointing to the dressing rooms!!! By the time Gary has collected his spare goalkeeping gloves and 'Steels' cap from inside his goals and then sauntered off the pitch! Everyone is not the wiser. Not even Gary himself! Why 'as he been sent for an early bath?

As the half time catering staff are kept busy feeding and watering the crowd, the mystery as to why 'Steels' loyal stalwart Gary Minton has been given his marching orders for the first time ever in his long career is solved. Mr Jack

Burroughs's explanation is soon revealed and that is he sent the lad off 'For Being Too Good'!!!. This amazing revelation is still the talk of Steelsbridge to this day!

In the second half of Gary's testimonial, Jack Burroughs's is found to be sat in the home dug out with his thick black overcoat pulled up at the collar. He is clutching and very much enjoying a steaming hot meat and potato pie. His blue woollen gloves folded around the pie! Jack had fixed up a suitable replacement, however.

Aimee Joyce made sure the second half of Gary's testimonial was a serious game of football. Her chance had finally arrived to take charge of a match with Jack Burroughs's saying he needed a breather! She kept up easily with the play throughout the half and was firm yet fair in her handling of the game!

The Man of the Match was never in doubt! The performance from the lad who had so nearly made the 1966 World Cup squad. Blazing down the left wing, Charlie Thorn set the match alight. His crossing was exquisite the way he caressed the football with pin point passes into Goldman and Sharpe had the capacity crowd in raptures! All clapping, cheering and stamping their feet! Almost lifting the roof from Linden Park! Gary Minton was redundant in the 1966 Legends goal. He was applauding and learning, even with his retirement looming about his goalkeeping trade still from his great friend Simon Clifton in the opposite goal, who was so assured and commanding and making some tremendous saves!

With just the five minutes to play, the crowd could not hold themselves back any longer. Aimee even signalled for a mass of yellow and blue fans to invade the Linden Park pitch.

Youngsters, teenagers, elderly men and women who thought they had seen it all supporting 'Steelsbridge Town' were now singing and dancing all over the Park's turf!

The England World Cup Select 0 Steel All Stars I was a perfect result for Gary Minton at his testimonial that sultry July night! Gary had scored the winner on what was is 650th and final outing for his beloved 'Steels'.

After being carried out of the Linden Park Stadium and then up the road to his Local Gary celebrated and celebrated and celebrated in The Shakespeare Tavern. Hundreds of customer's inside and out of Frank Taylor's 'Boozer' hailed Gary Paul Minton. The longest serving player in their football club's history well into the next day of Friday 7th July 1985!

The very end!